WHEN ALIENS PLAY TRUMPS

RUTH MASTERS

When Aliens Play Trumps
by Ruth Masters

First published 2013, re-published June 2023

ISBN: 9798387035357

Originally published under the author's previous name, Ruth Wheeler

Cover by Tim Hirst

PROLOGUE

Tom Bowler opened his eyes, rolled over and fell back into a deep slumber. His dreams were a rich tapestry of images.

The tapestry contained threads of Truxxe's service station Truxxe Superior Services, running through a patchwork of images of his home, Earth. He could see his parents, Fiona and James. They were in their tidy suburban house going about daily activities. The aroma of baked banana bread had been plucked from his memory. He walked from the hallway to the kitchen. The warm, sweet scent was intensifying with each step. Once in the kitchen, he encountered his cousin Max and his best friend Nathan. He remembered that Nathan wasn't on Earth, however - he had spent the last few months on Truxxe. Dream-state Tom pondered this for a moment, and then pondered his *own* presence on Earth. Wasn't he on Truxxe too? What was he doing in his parents' kitchen? And why was Kayleesh, his beautiful girlfriend from Augtopia there too? It seemed a little early in their relationship for him to be introducing her to his parents.

Tom Bowler's corporeal body fidgeted and flipped in the malleable ergonomic bed; in Tom's bed on the planet Truxxe. It had been an eventful gap year. Tom had left his parental home for a job serving burgers at an intergalactic service station, discovered the secrets of the planetoid on which he now lived and had been exiled to the deadly prison planet Porriduum. He had escaped the prison planet in question, with the help of his friend Raphyl's parents, after he and his friends had recovered them from a three-hundred-year cryo-sleep.

He had a job, good friends, a girlfriend and was a member of one of the best Spotoon teams on Truxxe. Life was perfect. Wasn't it?

But something was nagging at his brain. There was something he was supposed to remember. *Something important.* After Tom's triumphant return from Porriduum the previous rotation, he and his welcome committee had gone out to celebrate; obviously. That would explain his pounding head. It was also the most likely reason that his memory was so blurred. Tom pressed his fingers to his forehead, scrunched up his eyes, willing the memory to return fully formed. What was it? Was it something good? Something bad?

Paaaaaaaaaaaaaarp! The alarm rang through the building, calling the service station's employees to work. Tom swiftly washed, dressed in his work robe and grabbed a breakfast bar on his way out of the door. A lift full of workers took him from floor thirty-two, the employee living quarters level, to the ground floor where he alighted. The station was already bustling with activity as he made his way to the Express Cuisine where he worked. He found a troubled looking Kayleesh keying the activation code into her till. But when she noticed Tom, she greeted him with one of her incredible smiles. Tom couldn't resist a quick cuddle and a kiss on her soft, pale lips. Her soft, golden hair fell onto his face as he pulled her close. He breathed in the cinnamon scent he would never tire of. He pulled away from her, still detecting a touch of anxiety in her pretty face. He frowned.

"Is everything all right?" Tom asked.

"Yes, I think so."

Not quite believing her, he went to question her again, but a customer appeared at the counter. Judging by the size of him, Tom did not want to be one to get in the way of this man and his food.

"Twelve burgers and six ruffleberry milkshakes please," he barked. "And my wife will have the salad."

As the morning drew on, Tom desperately tried to remember whatever it was he'd forgotten. By the time lunchtime arrived, he was resigned to the fact that it was just an illusion. It was simply suitcase syndrome - the feeling one gets when packing for a holiday, that surely at least one item had been forgotten; an important item. And Tom knew that feeling only too well. He shrugged off the uneasy hunch and busied himself with his work. Raphyl and Nathan kept him amused with their antics, which were frequently quashed by the presence of their android supervisor Miss Lolah. Miss Lolah was a pherobot, whose very presence influenced her male employees to conduct themselves well in the work environment, work more competitively and therefore more efficiently. Raphyl had worked in the Express Cuisine for a number of years but he was still pliable in the presence of Miss Lolah, much to his aggravation. Kayleesh normally giggled to herself as she witnessed her colleagues react to the pherobot, falling over themselves to please the outdated and sexist construct of their supervisor. But today she seemed distant.

Once Miss Lolah had retreated to her office and her field of influence had waned, Tom approached his girlfriend. He took her hand and asked her once more whether she was OK.

"Tom, it's hard to explain but I keep thinking that there's something I've forgotten. Something too awful to remember – like some kind of temporary amnesia. Oh, I don't know. Maybe it was just a dream," she said, dismissively.

"You too?" Tom didn't know whether he should feel relieved or worried. The two emotions jostled for first place.

"You mean, you've been feeling the same way?"

Tom nodded. He squeezed her hands, in a bid to comfort her.

"Let go of her. She's not going to float away, Tombo," Raphyl chuckled.

"Raphyl," Tom said, seriously. "Can you remember what happened last night?"

"We went to Bar Six Seven, had a few drinks, played some spotoon; the usual." He shrugged.

"No, no. *Why* did we all go out and get so drunk?"

"Tombo, that is the most stupid question you've ever asked. I thought you were supposed to be intelligent?"

"Only for a human," Nathan piped up.

"What Tom *means* is *what happened?* What was it that was so dreadful we had to escape from? What happened *before* we went to the bar? Tom and I seem to have blocked it out!"

"Oh, you mean when Tom returned from Porriduum? Er, let me think," Raphyl pondered with the urgency of a sloth waking on the Sabbath. "Everyone was welcoming him back… and then Gracer's hologram appeared through the holoceiver… she muttered something about Radiakka invading Earth… people were chatting and then we all got burgers on the way home." Raphyl gave a tired smile and looked at the pair as though he'd just read out a shopping list.

"Rewind a bit there," Tom said. "Gracer… Gracer told us… of course! That was it! I *knew* it was something horrific!"

"She's not *that* bad looking. In fact, I rather…"

"Not *Gracer*," Tom snapped. "Gracer's *news* – Radiakka are about to invade Earth. What the *hell* are we doing fooling around serving burgers?"

Kayleesh gasped. A look of terror reigning her face as recollection hit her.

"Raphyl, why didn't you say something?" Tom asked, exasperated.

"I didn't think it was that important," he shrugged. "And anyway, why is it *my* responsibility? It's *your* planet. Why didn't *you* remember?"

"I don't know," Tom said quietly. "Perhaps it's what Kayleesh said – temporary amnesia – the notion is just so awful to contemplate so…we blocked it out."

"Humans really are strange," mused Raphyl.

"Hey I'm not human," said Kayleesh.

"Practically – you're dating one." He winked.

"What's going on here?" Nathan handed five milkshakes to a customer with as many hands and joined his colleagues.

"You must have forgotten too." Tom sighed. He explained the awful truth to his fellow Earthling.

"How could we have forgotten that?" Nathan's look of shock and confusion reflected his own.

"Temporary amnesia," Raphyl, Tom and Kayleesh said in unison.

"Well what are we doing serving burgers?" Nathan asked, hopping over the counter. "Let's go and save the Earth!"

CHAPTER 1

Raphyl, Nathan and Kayleesh were sitting around on the pliable ergonomic seats in Tom's apartment as Tom paced the floor.

"How are we going to do this?" Tom asked, half to himself. "We need to stop the Radiakkans. We need to contact Gracer. We need a spaceship, we need an army, we need…"

"You need to calm down!" Kayleesh said. "We can't have any of those things. We can't even afford to use the holoceiver to contact Gracer if we stop working at the Express Cuisine."

"And they'll never let all of their burger boys (and girls) be absent at once, will they?" Nathan questioned.

"I don't *care* about the burgers. All I care about is saving my home. *Our* home."

"I know," Kayleesh said, softly. She paused for a moment. "I have tried to contact the Submians Hyganty and Frarkk. After all, they helped us discover the secrets of Truxxe and helped us rescue you from Porriduum. But they're conspiracy theorists, not soldiers. Plus, they're out on another mission. They're three galaxies away, working undercover on some distant planet."

"I feel so helpless," Tom said.

"Me too," Nathan sighed. He sunk lower into his chair which bowed beneath him and accommodated his form.

"But *this* is your home now Tombo," said Raphyl. "Why are you always so interested in other planets?"

"Earth will always be my home, Raph," Tom said. He noticed his friend took slight offence to this, so he tried to explain. "I know you were never interested in your own planet, but that was when you were all alone, Raphyl. You were three hundred years away from your family, so you knew you could never get back. But now that you have them back, would you really want to be separated from your parents again? Would you really want them to be destroyed, your homeland? The people you care about?"

"I think I understand," Raphyl replied. "I'm sorry. I'll help you save your odd little planet if you like. Beats serving burgers."

Tom smiled.

"Besides, I think I know how we can fund this operation."

"You do?" Kayleesh grinned, unreservedly hopeful.

"I was thinking about it before. My parents were frozen on the cryo podiums for three hundred years. Their savings accounts must have accrued tonnes of interest during all that time. Am I wonderful or am I wonderful?"

"You *are* wonderful, but unfortunately your plan isn't," said Kayleesh. "Don't you remember why your parents were frozen in the first place? They were heavily indebted to the Radiakkans for the money they borrowed from them for their grand architectural projects. They couldn't escape when the Radiakkans froze them and made them trophies for all the universe to see, in the grounds of one of the very buildings they designed. They're broke, Raphyl."

Raphyl looked crestfallen.

"*My* parents, however, *do* have savings," Kayleesh beamed. "They spend all their time travelling from camp to camp with their travelling er ... show. They don't get chance to go out and spend it. They don't even have to pay any rent."

"But didn't you run away from Augtopia?" Tom asked.

"Well, I ran away from the family business yes," She said, unconsciously rubbing her chin. "But I'm sure my family would help out a friend of mine. Especially a friend as special as you." She put an arm around Tom.

"Before we all drown in our own vomit, shall we pool our money and get Kayleesh an appointment with the holoceiver so she can speak to her family?" Nathan interjected, never the one for public displays of tenderness.

Much to Nathan's disappointment, his work-shy nature almost beating Raphyl's, the four of them returned to the Express Cuisine the following rotation to work the day shift. As frustrating as it was, with Earth in peril and so very far away, there was little else that could be done until Kayleesh had spoken with her parents. And Tom knew only too well how it wasn't simply a matter of punching a number into a mobile device and waiting for a calling tone. Tom and Kayleesh wore timepieces on their wrists, which tripled up as communication devices and distress beacons in times of distress, but Kayleesh's parents didn't possess such contraptions. So, the only option was to communicate through the holoceiver creature, the same way Tom had on several occasions with his own family.

His own parents didn't know that when Tom visited them, his presence in their house was merely a hologram of their son, projected through a psychic, globular, transparent alien which was being transmitted from a distant planet. Fiona and James believed that their son was working at a motorway service station in South Devon to earn some money during his gap year. It wasn't a complete lie. They were just a few million light years out; more Extra-Terrestrial than Exeter.

Tom pondered whether E.T. seemed to find it easier to phone home than he did; where was a nineteen-eighties Speak and Spell, an old coat hanger and a foil-wrapped umbrella when he needed them?

The waiting list for using the popular method of communicating via the holoceiver creature was rarely under a week; ten Truxxian rotations. A hundred long hours.

When the day finally arrived, Tom, Nathan and Raphyl waited nervously in the waiting room at the Holoceiver Exchange. As daunting as a doctor's waiting room, but with more likelihood of seeing a saucepan-shaped head than a saucepan *stuck* on a head, Tom stared at the bleak walls. He sighed. What was taking Kayleesh so long? He imagined what was happening in the booth on the other side of the door. Kayleesh's body would be encased inside the creature, her mind and image projected on her home world of Augtopia. She would be talking to her family through the yellow-tinged bubble-skin of the creature for the duration of the call. He crossed his fingers, hoping that they would comply and find it in their hearts to help fund their mission. This would only be the first step of the plan, of course. He wasn't convinced that even the clever Kayleesh had an idea of what they should do next. Tom found himself wishing that Hyganty and Frarkk, the Submian creatures who resembled praying mantises, were able to assist them. What they lacked in looks, they made up for in intelligence, experience and ideas. Plus, they happened to own a pretty nifty spaceship which was just begging to be used in a war-like situation. It was even camouflage green. The long wait had evidently exceeded Raphyl's attention span as a lilac head slumped onto his shoulder, dribble already dripping onto Tom's compsuit.

"Raphyl!" he scolded. "I'm not a pillow."

"Wh... wh... what?" Raphyl sat upright, or as upright as Raphyl ever sat. he wiped at his chin, sleepily.

"Stay awake, can't you? She can't be *too* much longer."

"There she is," Raphyl mouthed.

Kayleesh couldn't have exited the booth yet, Tom would have heard the door. He had practically tuned his ears into the exact frequency for the eventuality. He was on high alert. But Raphyl had not meant Kayleesh. Tom turned to see Gracer Menille in front of them.

"Gracer," Tom stood up in surprise. "We've been waiting to hear from you." He wanted to say more but stopped himself. He did not wish for half of TSS to learn of their plight. He was about to suggest they talk somewhere quieter when his ears pricked up to the sound of the booth door opening.

A scream.

But the scream was coming from neither Kayleesh nor Gracer. The perpetrator of the scream was the receptionist. The small, bubble-like hollow-bodied receptionist somehow portrayed the look of sheer horror on her feature-less face. Tom supposed that the station's ALSID (Atmospheric Linguistic Spectrum Interpretation Device) unit had translated her fearful expression to make sense to him. He turned to see the object of her fear and saw that the holoceiver creature, normally tucked safely in the next room, was making its way into the waiting area.

"Get that out of here!" The reception yelped at Gracer. "Get it away from the other holoceiver!" But it was too late, for the door was now wide open and the creature was advancing towards Gracer's hologram.

CHAPTER 2

"What's happening?" asked Tom.

"Our holoceiver can sense the other one. *Get it away!*" The receptionist shrieked.

Gracer Menille was seemingly petrified, however, as her hologram remained static.

"Gracer, run!" Kayleesh yelled.

But the holoceiver was now almost upon her. Its voice resonated in Tom's brain. Soft and low.

"You're beautiful. Stay with me."

"Er..." Gracer managed.

"It's not talking to you, girl."

Tom noticed that it was trying a different method of communication, a more universal method, as it reached out with its limbs. He wasn't certain, but Tom got the impression that it was trying to mate with the semi-physical presence of the other psychic being that Gracer was in. Gracer had apparently come to the same conclusion and had found the strength to attempt an escape because her hologram ran out of the Holoceiver Exchange and down the passageway. Her holoceiver was thankfully obeying her wishes. Before her pursuer could reach the doorway, Nathan and Tom were already there, blocking the exit.

"Keep away from her," Tom warned. He doubted that his heroic façade would fool a being which could see into his very psyche, but it was worth a try. And it was definitely worth the look on Kayleesh's face, as she watched her brave boyfriend in action. Or it would have been, had the creature not stepped forward and enveloped him.

"Right, that's it," the receptionist barked. "I've warned you before, you're fired!"

"You can't fire me, I'm your brother!" The holoceiver approached the receptionist and completely failed to bang his fist on the desk. Tom sighed with relief as he was freed from the creature.

"That is irrelevant. I *got* you this job and I can *fire* you. I thought it would help you fight your... urges... but you're as bad as ever. Now get out!"

"Excuse me," Tom raised his hand, pathetically, "but is that a good idea? If he goes out into the corridor then he might be exposed to my friend again and -"

"And *you* can get out too. The *lot* of you!" Her voice seemed to bellow inside his brain. "Your friend is lucky I don't *fine* her for breaking the rules. I don't know... bringing another holoceiver so close to another exchange indeed..." she muttered. Tom didn't stay around long enough to listen to her finish. He, Kayleesh and Nathan were already halfway down the passageway, Raphyl lumbering behind them.

"Well that's put me off ever using one of those again!" Tom said.

"There's Gracer," Nathan pointed out. Gracer's hologram, already fading, was sitting inside a coffee shop, looking longingly at the pastry counter. He empathised with the girl who had the largest appetite of anyone he'd ever known, with the baked goods mocking her, thousands of light years from her taste buds. She was soon distracted, however, when Kayleesh sweetly asked her how she was.

"I'm fine," she replied. "I can't say I've ever experience anything like that before, though. And I shan't want to again!"

"It was quite funny, though," Raphyl winked.

"You would say that." Kayleesh rolled her eyes and suggested he bought the four of them a coffee to make up for it; minus the pastries, for it would be cruel to eat them in front of Gracer.

"I managed to get in contact with my parents," Kayleesh announced. "They are willing to lend us their new spaceship. In fact, they're on their way here now. It's nothing fancy, only a previously owned Augtopian –" Her words were broken by a kiss. She giggled. "I take it that you're pleased with the news then, Tom?"

"So, what is the plan?" Gracer asked. "To fly all the way to Earth in a second-hand spaceship, assuming you arrive before the planet has been invaded and/or destroyed, and somehow force the Radiakkans to leave?"

"Well it's the *start* of a plan…" Kayleesh looked a little hurt.

"And every one of Kayleesh's plans end in success!" Tom declared.

"As do mine," said Gracer.

"Exactly. Even if they are a little… unorthodox. So, with all of us together, we can't fail!"

"Coffee time," said Raphyl, returning to the table with four steaming cups. "They don't serve Truxxian Gloop here. Shame."

"Anyway, the reason I called you was to inform you about the situation on Radiakka."

"Be careful, Gracer," Nathan warned, blowing on his drink. "Discussing topics of a… er… *sensitive nature* can seriously get you into trouble. That's how I ended up here!"

"Serendipitous as that was, Nathan's right," Kayleesh said. "Don't discuss anything political if you can help it. Not while inside a psychic creature. Especially one on *Radiakka.* Which is where I assume your real body is?"

Gracer nodded and looked around the fading bubble which encased her. "Well if it's already heard my thoughts, I won't be much better off if I *don't* tell you anything. Besides, a whole planet is at stake here. Billions of people!"

"Gracer, you're brilliant," Tom beamed.

"I work inside the Wheylandian Parliamentary Building, as you know. It's where all the big decisions are made for the entire Radiakkan civilisation. It's how I found out about Radiakka II in the first place. The project has a new name, however; *Project Earth.*"

"Oh, so they're deciding to keep the name then? How nice," Tom quipped.

"Unlikely. They'll just enjoy it all the more when it becomes Radiakka II."

"Well, we're not going to let that happen!" said Kayleesh.

"I know," Gracer said, although she didn't seem very convinced. "Anyway, it seems that Earth has Radiakkans already living amongst the population. I don't think they're going for the all-guns blazing approach. It's as though they're planning on enjoying this take-over, taking their time."

"Which means we'll have plenty of time to stop them," piped up Raphyl.

"They'll be just as difficult to fight – we won't know how many of them there are, where they are, what they're doing..." Nathan sighed. "This is going to be impossible!"

"How can they be living amongst us... I mean, them?" Tom asked.

"I don't know. Unless they cover their indigo skin somehow. They're considerably larger than humans too, if you two are prime samples of your species." She eyed Tom and Nathan in a way which made Tom feel rather uncomfortable.

"I would say that we're both rather slight compared to a lot of humans..."

"Speak for yourself, you scrawny git," said Nathan. "How long do you think they've been living on Earth, Gracer?"

"It's hard to say. No more than a few years I should guess."

"*Years?* You mean they could have been on Earth when we were there? Maybe even living next door?

"Most likely."

"I always thought there was something odd about Mr. Sanders at number sixty-three," mused Nathan - "Perhaps he has blue skin underneath that beard and wears a wig!"

"So how are they going to go about the invasion?" Tom asked, ignoring Nathan's comment.

"They'll most likely either get themselves elected, corrupt the existing governments or go straight to the people, spread doubt amongst the civilians."

"I think humans are doing a pretty good job of doing all that themselves," Nathan snorted. "All governments are corrupt, in my book, and most people have always been paranoid and doubtful about the way in which countries are led."

"No wonder you left!" Raphyl scoffed. "All those governments and all those conflicting laws on one planet... it's not right. I remember you telling me about the criminal system, Tombo. Instead of sending criminals to somewhere central like Porriduum, your planet is divided into lots of areas which attempt to deal with their own problems in different ways. Completely barmy."

"Maybe it is." Tom shrugged. "Perhaps it's an advantage though. Perhaps the Radiakkans will be surprised at just how difficult Earth's various cultures and authorities will be to infiltrate."

"Gracer, you're really fading now," Kayleesh said, pensively.

"I know. I'll call again – as I assume you won't be able to contact *me* until the TSS holoceiver has been replaced. Good luck!"

Gracer's image slowly melted away before them. Kayleesh downed the dregs of her drink, determinedly.

"Let's go and wait for that spaceship!"

Tom Bowler observed a TSS transit ship as it was being readied for take-off. Lilac-skinned Truxxians, with messy, purple hair, were handling crates laden with cargo and transporting them up the main ramp to the central dome. He cast his mind back to the first time he had ascended one such ramp on one such ship. His life had not been the same since. He had boarded the ship, his mind full of school, television and other Earthly matters, ready to seek adventure. And he had found it. Here he was, not even a year later, embarking on his biggest adventure yet; a quest to save the Earth. He longed to go back in time, to his younger self in the Job Centre reading the job advertisement. He would want to whisper to younger Tom,

"You won't believe the consequences of accepting that job!"

A small spaceship clattered to an undignified halt between two transit ships. It was a dull copper colour and had the appearance of a dented teapot. It also made an inordinate amount of noise, puffing away like a steam train. Tom thought it looked rather odd, juxtaposed between the vast TSS ships. To his surprise, Kayleesh started to run up to it.

"Dad!" She called. Tom, Raphyl and Nathan followed her. As they approached, a sleek, black spaceship of equal size to the puffing teapot landed neatly behind it.

"Leesh!" A tall Augtopian disembarked and wrapped his arms around his daughter. He turned to look at the other craft. "Ah, I see that our lift home has arrived in good time," he remarked.

Kayleesh gasped.

"Dad! You should have worn a compsuit!" She shook her head, as another Augtopian stepped out of the black ship. A female.

"Oh, you know we don't bother with such things as clothes!" The female called out, at unnecessarily high volume.

Tom did not know where to look. He was meeting his girlfriend's parents for the first time and they had emerged from alien spaceships, stark naked. He found himself confronting his past self again, in his imagination. This time he was whispering, "And by the way, you know how you thought meeting your *last* girlfriend's parents was awkward?"

Tom was thankful that, as Kayleesh had previously explained to him, her father was preposterously hairy and therefore most of his body was covered in a dark blonde carpet. But her mother was smooth-skinned and stood proudly before him, arms outstretched, bearing all. Tom felt his face redden and hoped that the newcomers would not detect his embarrassment. Kayleesh introduced her parents to each of them.

"This is Raphyl, Nathan and my boyfriend Tom. Everyone, this is my mum Pumice and my dad Basalt."

Tom stopped himself from spurting out "rock on" and just gave a simple 'hello." So *that* was where he had heard the name Kayleesh before. Tom thought back to a geology module his science course had covered. *Caliche* was a sedimentary rock. He smiled to himself at the realisation. He learned something new about his girlfriend every day. *I wonder what her sister was called; flint perhaps?* he chuckled to himself. If a third naked Augtopian had been there however, particularly a young female one like Kayleesh, Tom didn't think he'd be able to cope. He managed to fix his gaze on their faces, and smiled politely, as was his demeanour.

"*Good* to meet you, sir," his father said, earnestly. Kayleesh's mother smiled and nodded.

Tom's reply, which was slow coming anyway after the shock of being referred to as "sir", was stifled by one of Kayleesh's typical bursts of enthusiasm.

"So, who wants to pilot The Belemnite then?"

"I do!" Nathan volunteered. His grin was wider than a Truxxian's. Kayleesh looked at Tom and Raphyl in turn.

"Is that all right with you two?"

"Fine by me," Tom said. "I've already had a turn at flying a spaceship. Let Nathan have his turn."

"Fine by me too," Raphyl shrugged. "As long as I can fly it back."

"Deal." Nathan beamed.

"Well then let me give you a quick crash course," Basalt offered. Tom wondered whether the term of phrase basalt had chosen was born from wit or coincidence. Basalt didn't smile, and it was difficult to read him, despite the influence of the ALSID. Basalt lead Nathan and Raphyl onto the ship.

"It was lovely to meet you all," said Pumice. "But I hope you'll excuse me as I need to return this beauty to its owner shortly," she said, eyeing the other craft. "We've already been a lot longer than I promised. Truxxe is further away than I thought. I'll start her up and wait for your father inside, Leesh. See you soon. And stay safe." She gave her daughter a meaningful hug and made her way back to the ship.

"I will Mum. Bye," Kayleesh called after her.

"It's not as easy as it looks." A huffy looking Raphyl emerged from the ship. "I haven't encountered much Augtopian technology before and this ship is *ancient*."

"Excuses, excuses." Kayleesh shook her head. "I wonder how Nathan's getting on. He has a longer attention span than you, Raphyl." She giggled as she boarded the ship.

"She's right, Raph," said Tom.

"She's right about what? I wasn't listening."

"You seem to have picked up the basics. I'm sure you'll be fine." Tom could hear Basalt's voice grow clearer. He appeared in the doorway and jumped down from the ship. He peered his head back through the doorway again and Tom avoided looking at the man's bare behind. Basalt's voice echoed into the ship. "Now all you have to do is press that button. Not that button, *that* button."

A rushing, whirring sound immediately rose, a spate of air and a grinding of engines.

"Not *yet!*" But Basalt's protestations and flailing of arms were ineffectual against the rising of the hull door and he quickly ducked out before his head and hairy body were emphatically parted.

"Stop them!" Tom gasped. "They can't go without us!"

"Come back," Basalt jumped up and down, fruitlessly. "Use the pedals!" But it was too late, for the craft was already half a mile away, wobbling towards the space port exit like a Skoda in a washing machine.

CHAPTER 3

"Nathan! What did you *do?*" screamed Kayleesh.

"What? I only followed instructions, I just pressed the button!" he protested, clinging onto the console.

"My stupid father," Kayleesh cursed. She peeled herself away from the wall and managed to negotiate her way to one of the flight chairs. Nathan fell clumsily into the chair behind him, losing his balance, and almost losing his breakfast too. Eventually both passengers were seated and struggling with their restraints in zero gravity. Once safely buckled in, Nathan let out a sigh of relief and instinctively reached for Kayleesh's hand and gave it a reassuring squeeze. They were safe. For now. He gazed at the screen above the console. Truxxe Superior Services was merely a glowing speck on the dark, shrinking planetoid.

"Kayleesh," he uttered.

"Yes?"

"Well that's a relief."

"What is?"

"I just wanted to check that there was some kind of ALSID on board. It's bad enough being stranded in space without being stranded with no kind of communication. I should know. I've been on a long-haul flight with my Nan. She is fluent in only gibberisheese."

"Actually, I am having doubts as to whether the ALSID is actually working because I can't understand a word of what you're saying," Kayleesh giggled. "And anyway, we're not stranded in space."

"We're not?"

"Of course not. Because you're going to pilot the spaceship."

"Well at least one of us has some confidence in me!" Nathan nibbled his lip as he looked down at the bank of controls.

"What are we going to do, Raphyl?"

"I don't know, Tombo. Pub?"

"I hope you're joking!"

"No. Well… yes of course I am." Tom wasn't sure whether or not to believe him. His mind was racing. Were Nathan and Kayleesh coming back for them? And if not, how were they going to get to Earth now?

"I hope they look after my ship," Basalt huffed.

"I hope the ship looks after them!" Tom snapped. "I'm sorry, but my friends are in there and we're stuck here with no way of getting to Earth! But... you have another ship, don't you? Could you drop us off?"

"I don't run a taxi service," Basalt snarled. His face softened. "We *could* offer you a lift, but unfortunately the craft my wife and I have borrowed only accommodates two travellers. Besides, I trust that my daughter will be safe with your friend for the time being."

"How convenient," Raphyl muttered.

Tom was beginning to understand why Kayleesh had fled her planet. Her family seemed loving enough, but how could they be so selfish as to shrug off the situation? Their daughter could be in danger. His planet was in peril.

"I don't think you understand, Basalt. My home planet is at risk. It's being invaded!"

"As are thousands of other planets in Triangulum and Andromeda alone! You're talking about The Milky Way! I'm sorry Tom, but what else can I do? I've lent Leesh my only ship and Pumice and I have already made the sacrifice of not attending tonight's performance."

"Of course. Your precious circus." The words tumbled out of his mouth before he could stop them.

"I beg your pardon? Young man, you and your kind need to learn some manners and appreciate..."

"My *kind?* You're beginning to sound like a Radiakkan!"

"Er Tombo..." Raphyl warned. "I think you went too far!"

"You're damn right he went too far!"

A sudden loud blast emitted from the shiny, black ship like the car horn of an impatient mother at the school gates.

The two Augtopians angered him so much that the temperature of Tom's boiling blood was reaching Vindaloo altitude.

"So, you're off then?" Tom snapped. "Back to Augtopia to forget about your daughter who has been flown light years away from her boyfriend in an old teapot?"

"Judging by your behaviour she's better off separated from you!"

"Why are you talking to me like I'm a child? I'm a grown man! *I've* escaped Porriduum!" Tom regretted the revelation as quickly as he said it.

"A criminal eh?" Basalt rubbed at his long chin. "Then she's definitely better off without you."

"I'm *not* a criminal," Tom protested, frustration ruling him. He opened his mouth to explain, but Basalt turned away and marched to the awaiting spaceship, simply muttering a rather loud,

"Humph!"

"Can you believe that man?" Tom gaped.

"It's probably not the *best* first meeting of your potential in-laws," said Raphyl.

"Understatement of the millennium. I just can't believe it. How could he be so... anyway," Tom resigned himself. "I will focus on our main problem, not on unreasonable beings. How are we going to get to Earth now?"

"Poor Tom," Kayleesh said, sadly.

"I know, I'm so sorry that we left him behind," Nathan said, glumly. "And Raphyl too."

"Worst still, I left him in the company of my father."

"I'm sure he'll get over the whole naked thing. He's not very judgemental, our Tom."

"It's not *that,* Nathan. You see, my father can be very self-centred. Tom will only have to say one thing he disagrees with and he can flip. And I'm not sure Tom could handle that."

"I think Tom's braver than you think. He's certainly a few shades bolder than before he came to Truxxe!"

"Maybe." Kayleesh viewed the monitors and sighed. "I was hoping that we'd see that other ship following us by now. It's obvious that my parents didn't see it in their hearts to bring Tom and Raphyl to Earth after us. They're so very selfish."

"Don't be upset. They'll find a way, I'm sure," he reassured her, his eyes never leaving the controls for a moment. "If he escaped Porriduum then he can leave Truxxe!"

"That was with the help of Raphyl's parents. Hey, do you think that they would be able to help? Raghael and Mirrie? They're still on Truxxe."

"I'm sure they'd be willing to, but I don't recall them mentioning owning a spaceship."

"That's a good point. I feel a bit useless just sitting here. Shall I make us some sandwiches?"

"That's the best news I've heard all day!"

"I wish Gracer was here," Tom sighed as he sipped a cool pint of lager. Raphyl had managed to persuade him to visit the recreational floor's Bar Six Seven after all. "It's like being back at home where none of my friends have cars. I never thought that I'd be complaining that none of my friends have spaceships. It all seems rather odd!"

"You say the strangest things, Tombo."

"Did I just hear you correctly?" It was Ghy Hasprin, the leader of Tom's spotoon team. He joined the bewildered looking pair at their table. "None of your friends have spaceships, you say?"

"Ghy! You don't happen to have one, do you? Or Mayty or Ransel or any of the other members of Hasprin's Legion?"

"Just how rich do you think we spotoon players are?" Ghy chuckled. "No, I do not own a spaceship but there is a way that we could possibly get one."

"There is?"

"If I said that where you need to get to could be within spitting distance, would you understand?"

"Does this have something to do with spotoon by any chance?"

"Hasprin's Legion is going on tour, Tom. That's what I came over to talk to you about. I'm sure we could play a game or two on whichever planet you need to visit. It's a popular game."

Tom's shoulders fell.

"I'm not sure it's very popular on Earth. In fact, I can guarantee that it's not."

"Earth eh?"

"Earth, soon to be Radiakka II."

"Radiakka II?"

"The Radiakkans are invading Tom's home planet," Raphyl said, matter-of-factly, before taking a swig of his potent Truxxian Gloop.

"I see." Ghy digested this information for a moment. "Well I'm sure we can still stop by."

"*Stop by?*" Tom felt his anger rising once more. "Why does no one else take this as seriously as me? My home planet is in imminent danger!"

"He's been like this all day," Raphyl said, shaking his head. "Don't take it personally, Ghy. He's very protective over his home world."

Tom sighed. "*OK,* I get it that Earth is only one planet of millions and billions, but it is important to me and if anything happens to my family, I don't know what I'll do."

"Quite right," Ghy nodded. "Then we'll do what we can."

"Thank you."

"I'll take it to the organiser and add Earth to the list. We're no longer playing on the second moon of Scorb as it has recently been occupied by terrorists from Scarla Nine, so I will suggest that we go to Earth instead."

"See what I mean?" Raphyl said, mildly. "It's happening all the time."

Poor second moon of Scorb, Tom thought.

"Well you've missed quite a lot of practice," Ghy said, taking his weight on two of his huge, burly, burgundy arms once more. "Shall we have a game now?"

Tom nodded and greeted his three other team-mates, Truxxians Chazner and Ransel and his colleague Mayty Reeston. They performed their team greeting by cocking their ears at each other; a custom which still made Tom laugh. Tom sipped his drink as Mayty stepped up to the oche, the standard distance away from the spotoon board. The board was a disc of the approximate size of a dinner plate. A target, this one now a little faded, was painted on the board in orange, red and green. Players aimed to hit the green, centre circle by shooting spittle at it using their skill and saliva gland production. This ability was apparently a rare one amongst most species and Hasprin's' Legion was proud to have a human as a member of their team; humans being some of the most adept players. Mayty stretched his long, orange arms and flexed his fingers. He visibly swilled a mouthful of saliva around his teeth and then projected a dart of saliva directly onto the disc, just inside the red circle. Tom rested his drink on the table and he and Raphyl clapped and cheered with the rest of the team. They were playing opposite the Right Ons; the oddly named team that had won the Big Game several months previous. They were infinitely better sportsmen than rival team the BBs and seemed to have quite a following. Their team captain was an Augtopian with burnished, waist-length brown hair and eyes which were the same bright violet as Kayleesh's. He tucked his hair behind his elfin ears and wiggled his long chin, as he waited for the disc to be wiped clean by Ransel. Ransel had barely removed the cloth when the Augtopian scored a perfect green. Impressed, both teams cheered. The contented participant took his seat and Ghy gestured for Tom to step up to the chalked line. He was out of practice, for spitting was not encouraged on Porriduum, but he was happy to be at the oche again. The activity was temporarily distracting him from worrying about bigger matters.

"Go Tombo!" Raphyl shouted. Team-mates and spectators alike joined in with shouts of encouragement.

Just let me have this moment. Before I have to go and save the world.

Tom Bowler gathered the largest ball of spittle he could muster and directed it as best as he could at the board. His perfect green on green score was met with whoops and cheers. He couldn't help but smile.

"I think something is wrong with the ship."

"That's the *worst* news I've heard all day," Nathan garbled through a mouthful of fwenna-fowl egg and cress. "What are you trying to do to me, Kayleesh? What do you mean, *something is wrong with the ship?*"

"Look at the instruments!" Kayleesh scooted across the bridge of the Belemnite, indicating a small bank of lights on the control desk. "Should those lights be flashing brown?"

"How is that even possible?" gasped Nathan. "You know, I didn't even notice those lights before. If there *was* something wrong though, then wouldn't there be an audible warning? Some kind of alarm?" The lights began to flash on and off, desperately. Nathan started to panic.

"Would it help the situation if there was?"

"Well no, but...well...what colour were they before?"

"I don't think they were lit before." Kayleesh looked worried. "But brown alert is generally pretty serious!"

"I think I can see where that theory comes from," Nathan shifted uncomfortably in his seat, in an effort to suppress a potentially noisy emission. "So what do we do?"

"I don't know. Check the manual?"

"There's a manual?"

"I expect so, somewhere." Kayleesh hunted around the bridge, methodically.

"A manual might have been handy when we were swirling out of control out of the space port!"

"I seem to remember that we were too busy concentrating on holding onto the walls – and our stomachs – to thumb through a fifty-page booklet!"

"How do you know that it has fifty pages?" Nathan discarded his sandwich; his appetite having left him.

"Because I've found it! It was in here, next to the toilet paper." Kayleesh closed a cupboard containing miscellany and held the manual aloft.

"Of course!" Nathan quipped. He glanced back at the bank of lights. They were still flashing. He wasn't sure how, but they were definitely brown. Perhaps they were filled with some kind of gas. That notion seemed to make even more sense to him.

"It doesn't say anything in the manual about staring at the lights to make them go out," Kayleesh said.

"Hey, I was just checking them!"

"I know, sorry." Kayleesh flicked through the publication, seating herself as she did so. "Aha. Brown lights... here we are... coffee filter needs changing."

"Is that all?"

"Apparently so."

"Right. Shall I change it then?"

"I'll do it," Kayleesh shook her head. "If only to stop those damn lights flashing. But before I embark on such a perilous quest, I'll try and find the chapter which explains how to land this thing shall I?"

Tom Bowler was in his living quarters packing his rucksack with all the items he deemed necessary for his trip. He didn't have many possessions on Truxxe and the only things he had bought since his arrival were clothes, his timepiece and the wall-mounted Melody Mech. Tom looked at the sleek looking device on the far side of the modestly-sized apartment. He realised that he had not played any music on it since returning from Porriduum. If he hadn't bought it and illegally copied the Radiakkan music card, he wouldn't have experienced the horrors of the prison planet. Tom shuddered. He was on his way for a final visit to the sanitation room when there was a heavy knock on the door.

"Hello Raph," Tom said, and the foxglove skinned alien ambled in. He was carrying a holdall which he promptly rested on the table.

"Hello Tombo."

"I'm impressed!" laughed Tom. "I thought I'd have to come and wake you. Who are you and what have you done with Raphyl?"

"What are you talking about, Tombo? It's me!"

"I know, I was simply saying... never mind. Wait there, I'll be back in a krom."

"Are you sure it's all right for me to tag along on tour with your team?" Raphyl shouted through the wall.

"Yeah, Ghy said it's not a problem, I told you," Tom yelled back. "And I can't save the Earth on my own. I need as much help as I can get." Tom emerged from the bathroom, brushing his unruly hair. As he did so he examined his friend's crop of dark purple hair from across the room. "Although... I'm not quite sure how I'll explain you."

"How you'll *explain* me?"

"Here." Tom fished a beany hat from the depths of his rucksack. He threw it at Raphyl who shrugged and pulled it down over his hair and ears. "You don't want to shave off that monobrow do you? Or at least *some* of it?"

"No I don't! Did they make you *grow* one when you landed on Truxxe?"

"No, but Truxxe is used to seeing people of different shapes and sizes and species. Earth *isn't.*"

"Well isn't that *their* problem, not mine?"

"Well, yes, I know where you're coming from. But if they find out they're being invaded by people from another world before we can step in and stop it all happening, they're not going to look favourably on anyone that looks so *different.* I'm sorry. It's just the way it is there." He proffered one of his remaining two disposable razors.

"Very well," Raphyl took the razor and reluctantly headed towards the sanitation room. Tom continued to pack, scanning the room for anything he may have missed. He snorted to himself - he was really looking forward to seeing this! Raphyl emerged, the beany pulled down over his eyes. Tom advanced and re-positioned it, revealing Raphyl's new style. Laughter spilled out of him. Raphyl frowned and clapped his hands over his forehead, defensively. "Yes, now I look as stupid as *you*."

"Ah I'm sorry, Raph. You just look different that's all. Kind of like if you'd suddenly grown a moustache. But the opposite."

"I presume it still matters to you that I'm purple?"

"It might matter to other humans. But don't worry about that. My mum is always raving on about the local spray-tanning salon."

CHAPTER 4

Raghael and Mirrie waved as Tom and Raphyl ascended the ramp to the ship with Hasprin's Legion. Tom felt as though he was boarding a football team minibus at the school gates. But instead of a cramped, confined school bus full of sweaty school bullies, it was a lush, airy spacecraft full of sweaty aliens. And instead of a journey up the M42 to a town that was thirty miles away, a trip across the great expanse of space was laid out before them. Tom couldn't help but feel excited, despite knowing the real reason for the expedition. He had been reassured that the relative time between them leaving Truxxe and eventually reaching Earth would not be too great. The modern ship, with its speedy new system and FTL drive, meant that he wouldn't arrive home generations later. Or worse, generations of Radiakkans later.

Tom took a seat in a booth with Raphyl, Ghy and Mayty. He breathed in the newness of the interior and made himself comfortable. The brightly lit seat bay, with its plush furniture and backdrop of the universe through the window, was not an unpleasant place to be.

"Where are we going first?" Tom asked Ghy.

"Our first game is against a team based on Jaloosh; Candy's Comrades."

"Candy's Comrades?" Raphyl scoffed. He leaned back in his seat and hauled his legs onto the table. "You're playing against a bunch of girls?"

"Do not be fooled by their team name. Candy is one of the toughest and best spotoon players on Jaloosh!" Ghy said. "In fact, I hear that the whole team has a good skill set. Not a weak player amongst them."

"Well, neither do we," Tom sniffed.

"Exactly. We're well matched!" Mayty's grin spread across his huge, orange head.

"How did Hasprin's Legion afford the use of such a new ship?" Raphyl asked, clearly impressed.

"I applied for funding through TSS. I didn't expect to hear anything back, but our application was successful. They've even supplied a small crew to man it. There er... there is a catch though."

"A catch?" Tom asked.

"I'm afraid so. We have to wear these for every single match throughout the tour." Ghy heaved a sizeable sports bag onto the table and rummaged through it. He threw something wrapped in polythene at Tom, and another at Mayty. Tom tore open the packaging and a bright blue t-shirt flopped out. The letters TSS were adorned the expanse of material, both front and back, in bright silver.

"Not too subtle!" Mayty laughed, examining his own shirt.

"They're not too bad," Tom shrugged, holding it up to his torso. He noticed that the team name was embroidered onto the right shoulder.

"And that's not all. There is the headgear too."

"Are they like the caps that TSS employees wear? They're not so bad."

"They're not so much hats... as earmuffs."

It was time for Raphyl to laugh. As Ghy handed out bright blue earmuffs to the reluctant pair. Through the stares of horror from Chazner and Ransel across the room, Raphyl suddenly felt less self-conscious about his shaved monobrow.

By the time Hasprin's Legion's small ship landed, it was night-time in the northern hemisphere of Jaloosh. Raphyl happily slumped onto one of the bottom bunks in the sleeping quarters, despite having slept in his seat for most of the journey. Tom clambered onto the bunk above. A shiver ran down his spine as he recalled sleeping in a bunk bed back on Porriduum. But this was infinitely more comfortable, and at least he had friends here. There was also the added bonus of not risking losing a limb every time he moved so much as three feet from his bed. The idea of the deadly star, Gorgon, and its lethal rays which penetrated through Porriduum, forcing the prisoners to stay in their cells or else risk getting fried by the rays was still with Tom. The smell of burnt flesh from a neighbouring cell and an unfortunate sleep-walking inmate was one that would never leave his nose; and the sound that he made as his entire body burnt to a crisp, was one that would never leave his ears. Tears formed in his eyes, and remained there, as he drifted off to sleep.

Tom dreamed about Kayleesh. He dreamed that she was on Earth with Nathan who was introducing her to his parents and showing her around his home town; his school, his friends, his home. Next, the two of them were laughing and sharing a picnic in North Whitchall Park and enjoying the warm, summer sun. They were sitting close and Nathan was feeding her ruffleberries from a tin.

Tom woke up in an angry haze. How *dare* Nathan be having fun with Kayleesh. How *dare* he show off his town, *Tom's* town. It was Tom who was supposed to be with her, not him. He shook the irrational dream thoughts from his half-sleeping mind and clarity found him once more.

Then horror followed.

What if the Radiakkans had taken over by now? What if they had enslaved the human race? How safe were his friends and his family?

Stop it, Tom. He told himself. *Worrying is not going to solve anything. Nothing can be done until we reach Earth. Until then, Kayleesh and Nathan will just have to look after each other.*

How he longed for her.

Tom settled back down under the bedclothes and closed his eyes. He eventually drifted off to sleep, which proved quite a challenge in a room of alien males who now all seemed to be performing in some kind of unconscious orchestra of snores.

"Oh no my battery has nearly run out," Kayleesh sighed.

"Battery?" Nathan parroted. His gaze flickered between manual, control panel and screen.

"For my Interculator."

"Your what?" Nathan said, a little irritated. He was trying to concentrate on keeping the ship travelling in the right direction - and in keeping them alive. The navicomp indicated that they were travelling steadily. He allowed his eyes to leave the screen momentarily and glanced at the forlorn Kayleesh.

"This device." Kayleesh pointed to her wrist, the one on which she was not wearing her timepiece. Nathan hadn't noticed that she wore anything on that arm before. "It calculates how many calories I've eaten against how many calories I've burned. See, the red light is flashing, low power. And I don't suppose Earth has universal chargers?"

"Oh no, not more flashing lights," tutted Nathan.

"Hopefully it'll last a few more days or I'll have to use the old-fashioned route and write it all down."

"Seems a bit obsessive," Nathan said. "Anyway, why does a svelte creature such as yourself need to keep count?" He turned back to the screen.

"Well that's the point. I don't need to keep count with this. It helps me to maintain the same weight. Hopefully I'll get a few more rotations out of it before it switches itself off. It currently states that I have consumed one thousand calories today and burned one thousand three hundred. Which means… I can have another sandwich," she said, happily.

"You'd think that a device that clever would run on kinetic power rather than batteries. If its focus is on energy, then why doesn't it use some of yours to power it?"

"Ingenious!" Kayleesh giggled. "You see, this is why *you're* the one piloting the ship! You should contact Interculator Inter-Galactic. I'm sure they'd love to hear your idea."

"My idea? Well that kind of technology isn't my idea, but..."

"Ooh it's an Earth idea? I'm really looking forward to visiting your home world, Nathan. The more I hear about it, the more intrigued I am."

Nathan said nothing and re-read the paragraph on docking and landing for the fifteenth time. Kayleesh disappeared for a while, and Nathan presumed she had gone to make herself another sandwich. When she returned, she sat back in her flight chair and soon began to snore, softly. Nathan didn't mind missing out on sleep, but they still had some distance left to travel.

By the time Kayleesh awoke, it was some hours late and Nathan felt much more confident about how and where he was going to land the ship. He had set the manual down and blithely guided the ship as though he had been doing so for his entire career.

"Nathan?" she asked him, sleepily.

"Yeah?"

"Have you noticed anything different?"

"Er... like what? What's gone wrong now? Has the warning light gone off in the sanitation cubicle because we've run out of air freshener?"

"No of course not," she giggled. He turned to her. She looked the same, the ship looked the same.

"I give up," he shrugged.

"I've turned the ALSID off!"

"You've what? Then how..."

"I'm speaking your Earth dialect!"

"You are? How long has the ALSID been switched off?"

"Not that long. An hour or so before I fell asleep," she shrugged, casually.

"That's pretty impressive. And with skills like that you still work in a burger bar!"

Kayleesh laughed. "I love the way that that phrase translates,"

"Why? What does it sound like to you?" Nathan asked, curious. He corrected the ship's course slightly.

"It sounds a bit like our phrase for People Pie Place."

"Right," Nathan guffawed. Then added, "remind me *not* to set a course for Augtopia!"

Chazner and Ransel, the Truxxian members of Hasprin's Legion, were exchanging laughs and stares as they pulled on their over-sized team t-shirts and reluctantly pinged on the ridiculous bright blue earmuffs. Mayty's earmuffs were stretched absurdly over his bulbous, orange head and Tom couldn't look at the stocky, masculine Ghy without howling uncontrollably. The team disembarked the ship, a mass of bright blue and shiny silver, into a large, grey space port. The port was awash with an array of beings, most of whom appeared to be of the three-legged variety and sporting pointed heads and narrow eyes. Tom assumed that these were the natives of Jaloosh. Their high-pitched chatter rang above the noisy hum of the comings and goings of various spacecraft. Tom could make out occasional words as they greeted Ghy Hasprin, and the sound was as piercing and uncomfortable as dusty nails on a chalkboard. Tom was actually grateful for the earmuffs. The team followed a group of the natives as they lead them out of the port, along a high walkway above a bustling urban street and finally to the venue where the game was to take place. The room which had been allocated to the game reminded Tom of the kind in which a wedding reception would be held. But instead of balloon arches and bouquets, banners supporting both teams and photographs of both Hasprin's Legion and Candy's Comrades adorned the walls. Tom frowned for he did not remember ever posing for a photograph.

TSS has a habit of finding ways of scanning and manipulating the thoughts of people without them even knowing, Tom mused, as he considered the pherobots and holoceivers. *Taking sneaky photographs is probably a breeze by comparison.*

"It looks as though Candy's Comrades are an all-Jalooshian team," Tom murmured to Ghy, eyeing the photographs.

"*Jalooshives,"* Ghy corrected him. "Not only that, they're all female."

"You know you have to win this game, don't you, Tombo?" Raphyl grinned.

"I have a feeling you'll never let me live it down if we don't!"

A group of people, which could only have been Candy's Comrades, filed into the room. They were dressed in a significantly more dignified manner than Hasprin's shimmering motley crew. The team nodded and smiled politely at Tom's team before taking seats at the far side of the room. One of them remained standing, however; a girl with long, pink hair sprouting from all over her pointed head. She had her back to the room and gesticulated wildly as she spoke. Despite apparently keeping her voice to a low whisper, her screeches could be made out by everyone present - Candy was very blatantly giving her team a not-so-secret pep talk.

Ghy waved at his own team and gathered them together, before offering his own boost of encouragement. Raphyl's attention didn't lend itself to listening in, however and he sloped off to the bar.

"Well if no one's going to get the drinks in then I will."

A tall Jalooshive gave a piercing cough to gain the attention of the room.

"May I take this opportunity to thank you all for your attendance? There will be six rounds of the traditional game of spotoon this evening. Standard rules apply. First, I'd like to introduce our home team *Candy's Comrades.*" At which point, another group of Jalooshives entered the already full room. The group consisted of half a dozen female Jalooshives, dressed in matching outfits and rustling large, pink, pompoms.

"*Cheerleaders?*" Tom mouthed.

The girls treated their audience to an uncomfortably high-pitched chant, accompanied by a rather complex dance routine.

"Candy can do what you can't do, spits on the dribblers with her crew. C.A.N.D.Y. will keep on going 'til her mouth is dry."

"I don't think the ALSID did their chant justice," Chazner sniggered.

"And now be so good as to welcome our visiting team, all the way from the planetoid Truxxe, *Hasprin's Legion,"* the tall Jalooshive announced. Tom was even more surprised when the doors parted again, and yet more beings appeared, to the backdrop of applause. More cheerleaders. But these girls were different. Tom recognised one of them. In fact, he recognised *all* of them. They were all *Gracer Menille.* How could this be?

The girls bumbled through a brief dance routine, which included leapfrogs, cartwheels and hand claps. Their voices rang loud and clear; "Ghy Hasprin is no has-been, he has the best team and they are mean," they chanted in unison.

"Oh dear," Tom murmured and buried his face in his hands, cringing. What was Gracer doing here? And why were there six of her? And why had she chosen such a terrible song?

Tom was used to his friends inexplicably appearing on whichever planet he happened to be, light years from anywhere, but not in duplicate. The confusion did not bode well for Tom's concentration as he stepped up to the oche.

CHAPTER 5

"Well at least you won," Raphyl said, handing Tom a drink.

"But you didn't have to be so modest in front of the girls – you should have really gone for it. I've seen you play much better."

"I know," Tom sighed. He joined in the team signal with the others, cocking his ear in the air as was custom, before taking a seat with Raphyl. "But how could I focus when there were six Gracers staring at me?"

"Six Gracers?"

"The cheerleaders."

"What do you mean?"

"How are there six of them?"

"They're not all Gracer," Raphyl laughed.

"They all certainly look like her. They even have her smile. And no one else walks like that!"

"They all look like her because they're her children."

"They're her what?"

"Her hatchlings. I met Gracer at the bar and she told me she'd brought them along to cheer you on, Tombo."

"Tom!" One of the Gracer Menilles appeared, grinning at him.

"Gracer?" Tom wavered. He stood up to greet her.

"Yes, it's me. And I'm really here this time, not in a holoceiver." And by means of proof she reached out and hugged him. "We came to cheer you on."

"So I see. This is a surprise! More than I can express"

Gracer leaned in and whispered in Tom's ear.

"I'm sorry about the cheer!"

"Mum, is this really Tom?" One of the hatchlings bobbed around Gracer, excitedly.

"Yes, this is the man who was around when I laid your egg," she beamed.

"That's not how it sounds!" Tom shot a glance at Raphyl. "How you've grown!" he said, pathetically. He never did know what to say to children. Even if they were fully grown.

"Did you like our dance?"

"It was very good, yes," he said politely. For the girls were as graceless as their mother, despite her name.

"Why don't you go and get some ruffleberryade for all of you?" Gracer suggested and placed some coins in the girl's hand.

"Sorry, this is all a bit... strange," admitted Tom. "How did they grow so quickly? I mean... she was just an *egg!* And how many of your children are there?"

"They have to grow quickly," Gracer said. "I have so many of them that I can't possibly nurse them all indefinitely. This batch is just about ready to fend for itself."

Tom took a large swig of frothy Jalooshive beer. It was palatable.

"So how did you know to find us here?" Raphyl asked.

"I'm an avid reader of Sputum Monthly," she grinned. "The game was in the events listing so I thought, as Jaloosh is in the same solar system, I'd head here and meet up with you. It didn't cost too much on the solar express ship. I got a group booking, with the girls."

"So Jaloosh is in the same system as Radiakka? That's handy," said Raphyl.

"Handy?" Tom spat. "You mean to say we're on the doorstep of the race which are currently invading Earth?"

"Don't panic," said Gracer. "They won't be coming here. They'll be heading to Earth."

"That's really comforting, *thank you!*"

"I still can't believe you're talking in English," said Nathan.

"Well it will make things easier on Earth, won't it?"

"Absolutely. It's very cool."

"So I hear. I'm glad I packed a jumper," Kayleesh said, rifling through a knapsack.

"This is going to be fun." Nathan laughed to himself.

"Are we far from the docking station?"

"There's not exactly a docking station," said Nathan. "But we're about to go into Earth's orbit."

"How exciting!"

"And Earth does still seem to be here. Which is a bonus."

"How do the girls have their hair where you come from?" Kayleesh asked, as though it was of great importance.

"They wear it sort of up, Weena."

"Weena?"

"Never mind. Have you got a hat?"

"I've got this," Kayleesh held up a woollen garment that could pass for a beany hat.

"Perfect. Pull it down over your ears and you'll fit in just fine. Apart from the violet eyes, maybe. But you could pretend to be one of those girls who wear coloured contact lenses."

"I won't look like a freak then?"

"Kayleesh, you could never look like a freak." Nathan was satisfied that Kayleesh could pass for a human. A truly beautiful human at that. Tom was very lucky. "You might turn a few heads, but not for that reason."

Nathan focussed his attention back to the ship and concentrated on bringing it in to orbit. Where would he land the ship? He didn't want to draw any attention to it. He wished that it would fit in his garage or that he knew of somewhere he could easily conceal it. He hoped that he could utilise the cover of night, but it occurred to him that he had no idea what time it would be in England when they landed. And even then, they could be spotted. He tried to remember whether the craft was fitted with blinking, colourful lights which would easily startle onlookers below. Or maybe he'd inadvertently land in a field of fearsome Radiakkan spaceships. Nathan just did not know what to expect.

"I wonder if I can pick up the news on one of these screens?" Nathan mused. If he had an idea of the current situation on Earth, he would be at less of a disadvantage.

"You might be able to detect radio signals as we near the destination," suggested Kayleesh. She consulted the manual and adjusted some of the instruments on the control desk. A whistling, crackling sound emitted from somewhere. Nathan spotted a speaker above his head. Vague speech patterns started to filter through. Was it Russian? German? Languages were not Nathan's strong point.

"Can you go and put the ALSID back online? I'll keep twiddling."

The ALSID soon abided by its duty as a thick, German accent enunciated in perfect English through the crackling speaker.

"Buy today and pay nothing until the year two thousand!"

"Adverts," Nathan muttered. "Typical. The first transmission from Earth I've heard in months and it's a flaming advert!"

Kayleesh took over control of the dial as Nathan drew his attention back to the navigation system once more.

"...mass food poisoning epidemic which infected all five hundred cruise ship passengers..." A British accent announced.

"I think you found the news!" Nathan gestured for Kayleesh to leave the instruments as they were. The informative voice continued through the hissing speaker.

"...Seventeen passengers and three crew members are currently in a critical condition. Investigations of the situation are under way. Our other top story tonight is the brutal murder of two police officers found dead in Hyde Park..." the speaker let out a few crackles, and then settled to a low hiss. "The bodies of Inspector Benjamin Hardy and Constable Alan Johnson were discovered by dog walkers early this morning. They were found with bruises around their necks and their shoes had been removed.

Emily Swift, one of the women who was unfortunate enough to have found the bodies of the police officers, has described the scene as *disgusting and sickening. 'How anyone can take another person's shoes is just horrifying!'...*"

"I think that'll do," Nathan waved dismissively at Kayleesh. The hissing ceased.

"Do you think that told us anything?" Kayleesh asked.

"England seems the same as it was, if that broadcast is anything to go by."

"Well there was no mention of giant spaceships and indigo-skinned beings running riot with laser guns, I suppose," said Kayleesh.

"So where are we off to next?" Gracer asked.

"*We?* I'm not sure which planet the team are travelling to next but I'm not sure you can all..."

"We're your cheerleaders, Tom. Surely we can come along with our team?" Gracer's smile faltered, her lip almost visibly quivering.

"I'm sorry Gracer, but I'm not sure whether Ghy-"

"I'm sure Ghy will be fine with it, Tombo." Raphyl, suddenly oozing testosterone, slapped Tom's back. "It might balance things out a bit on board the ship!"

"Plus, when we *do* get to Earth, you'll have even more backup against the Radiakkans," said Gracer.

"Things are certainly looking up for this trip!" Raphyl gave one of his wide grins, winked and sank back into his seat, propping his feet on the drinks table.

"Surely you won't send your children out into a war zone Gracer," Tom protested.

"Of course not. We'll be an army of thinkers. It's what Menilles do best."

Tom threw his arms around Gracer for the second time that evening.

The trio joined both teams for affable conversation for the remainder of the evening. Tom waited until Ghy had drank enough of his intoxicating liquor of choice to turn his skin a paler shade of burgundy before broaching the subject of the cheerleaders joining them on tour. Ghy roared with laughter, raised a toast to Gracer and her daughters and happily allowed two of them to perch on his lap. He courteously congratulated them on their song and gave a rendition of the cheer himself.

"Ghy Hasprin is no has-been, he has the best team and they are mean." He laughed loudly, looking around the group for approval.

"Well remembered!" One of the hatchlings clapped her hands. Tom thought that he should try to learn their names, but he knew that he'd struggle to remember them all. It was challenge enough differentiating Gracer from her daughters and he'd known her for much longer. It was almost as though they were ageing before his eyes, developing and maturing.

Perhaps they will *be old enough to be soldiers by the time we actually get to Earth,* he mused. *They are such a fascinating race.*

"Where is our next destination?" Mayty Reeston asked Ghy, after his third round of the cheer.

"Unfortunately, we will have to leave the beautiful planet Jaloosh by daybreak," he said. "And then we're off!"

"Off where? Is Earth our next stop?" Tom asked, hopefully.

"Why not?"

Tom grinned.

Ghy Hasprin looked at his timepiece through one eye in an attempt to focus. The team captain grinned, raised his glass and announced,

"However, daybreak on Jaloosh is not for another fourteen hours!"

"I hope the ship medical box is kitted with abstemious pills!" Gracer whispered.

"I hope so, too," said Tom. He turned to Raphyl, who seemed to have been slapped with the stupid stick. A more stupid stick than normal. He followed his gaze and saw that he was observing two of the Menilles who were dancing several feet from the group.

"They're enchanting, aren't they?" Raphyl boozily verbalised.

"That's an interesting description, Raph." Tom regarded the females' moves which were as gauche as their vocals.

"Well, they are, Tombo. They're beautiful. All of them."

"Well you certainly seem to be under their spell!" Tom laughed.

Tom awoke from the little sleep he'd managed to achieve in the noisy bunk room. The discomfort of the discordant snores from the men's sleeping quarters had been supplemented by the squeals and giggles of excitable girls in the adjacent room. Didn't those Menille girls ever sleep? His head was ringing with the sound of the Hasprin's Legion cheer. Had they been signing it all night too or was his memory mixing with his dreams again?

Yawning, he pulled off his earmuffs, which he had continued to use as makeshift ear defenders and went out into the corridor. Bare feet on cold metal, he thought about the events of the evening before. In remembrance, the corners of his smile shook hands with his ears.

We're going to Earth next!

He padded along the corridor and found Ghy at the table in the area where they had been seated on the journey to Jaloosh. He was sitting alone.

"Ghy!"

"Ssh!" Ghy protested. "Can't you tell when a man has a bad head?"

"I take it there are no abstemious pills on board?" Tom asked, almost whispering.

"Unfortunately, not," Ghy sighed. "I'm sorry I shouted. Take a seat, Tom."

Tom sat opposite the hung-over team captain. He still looked pale and his eyes were sunken. Tom wondered why he was out of bed at all.

"I have a packet of fastacs in my bag. I can go and fetch them if you like," Tom offered.

"Thank you but no, I will suffer the consequences. It was foolish of me to have partied so heavily on the first night of the tour. I should have been more responsible; or at least checked the ship's medical supply in advance."

"So, when are we leaving for Earth?"

"Earth?"

"Yes. You said that we'd be on our way there at daybreak today."

"I did?"

"Yes, last night!"

"Last night was last night," Ghy said. He rubbed at his sore head with one of his muscle-bound arms.

"But-" Tom stood up, his teeth clenched in anger, fists tightening.

"Besides, Earth in not next on our course. We'd waste tonnes of fuel if we took a detour before continuing on our tour."

"The tour is all you care about!" Tom's temples were throbbing. He could feel his wrath grow inside him as though it was a ball of expanding foam. He could stand it no longer. He needed to let it out before rage consumed him. "And spotoon! Well, let me tell you *Ghy Hasprin,* there is more to life than spitting at a plate!"

Tom's face was growing as red as the creature he was confronting -

the huge, barely sober and *extremely strong* creature.

Tom felt as though he was having an out of body experience; the pale, slight human and the monstrously sized alien, whose arms were thicker than Tom's waist.

What am I doing?

He gulped.

And he ran.

"Tom, wait!" Ghy blared after him.

But Tom didn't wait.

But where would he go?

It was only a small ship.

Perhaps he could leave the ship.

He looked about him for the exit controls.

But it was too late. A heavy hand fell onto his shoulder.

"Tom! Come and sit down. I'm not going to hurt you. You're right. All I've thought and cared about these last few years *is* spotoon." Tom gingerly shuffled back to the table after him. "But there is a reason for that. It's my escapism."

"I see," Tom said, taking his seat once more.

"My brother Bhry is ill, Tom. He has been ill for a long time and now... and now he's deteriorating rapidly. He has not got long."

Tom's jaw slackened, and his eyes broadened. "I didn't know."

"No one knows. I came to Truxxe to get away from my troubles. I felt helpless watching him worsen day by day – so *powerless.* I moved into the service station and united a team to make something of myself and to make my brother proud of me – to give him something to smile about. I embraced spotoon and the lifestyle it entails even helped me to forget. Most of the time."

"Right." Tom was unsure of how to respond. He realised, in that solemn moment, that he knew a lot of people who had found comfort in escaping to Truxxe; Ghy, Kayleesh, Nathan, even himself.

"But your problem is bigger than mine, Tom. Your planet Earth is bigger than my world of spotoon."

"It's very important to me." Tom nodded.

"I can see how passionate you are about it." Ghy leaned in close, traces of intoxicating liquor on his breath. "I'm sure we can alter our course."

"Do you mean it?" Tom smiled.

"Earth, here we come!"

Nathan's now masterly command of the spaceship's controls traversed the Belemnite across the dusky countryside. Scanning the area, recognition sent his heart racing, and the perfect landing spot suddenly occurred to him. He drew the ship around in a smooth arc, heading towards the city. He knew it was a risk, but in only a few miles they would be concealed. They would be concealed in full view.

"Where are you taking us?" asked Kayleesh.

"To the Science and Discovery Centre. It's in the middle of the city. There's a permanent exhibition displaying man's view of other-worldly spacecraft throughout the ages. Tom and his cousin Max have dragged me along to it many times. It was a cheap day out during the long summer school holidays, a few sandwiches, a can of pop and a wander around the free exhibition. Part of it is outdoors, fenced off from the busy street. If we're lucky there will be enough space for this old thing."

"Sounds like a very peculiar place!"

"Well, yes I can see why you'd think that. But to us it was a kind of haven."

The sound of a police siren fading into the distance, and the increasing height of edifices did much to denote that they were close to their destination. The city looked so different from this view and Nathan struggled to make out the roads he was searching for from above. But he soon recognised the old Cathedral and the Post Office Tower, and it wasn't long before the caged area containing the Science and Discovery Centre's unique exhibits came into view on the screen.

"It's still there!" Nathan whooped. One hand leafing through the manual and the other dancing over the control desk, Nathan managed to lower the Belemnite into the makeshift docking bay. It landed with a puff and a clunk, but it had landed. His body coursing with adrenaline, Nathan powered down the ship and shakily got to his feet, as though he was disembarking from a full day on the waltzers. The two of them stepped out and squeezed past a silver-coloured imagining of a flying saucer on their exit. Its paint was flaking and its bodywork weather-beaten. Next to that a model of a rocket stood proudly, despite its rusty hinges and eroded nosecone.

"It's a shame they didn't look after this place a little better." Nathan frowned. He realised that he had landed in the now vacant spot which was once occupied by another model. "Oh, they've got rid of the Overlord ship. I used to like the Overlord ship." He read the now-redundant accompanying information sign. "It couldn't have been moved that long ago."

"At least the Belmenite doesn't look too out of place amongst this assortment," Kayleesh noted.

"Exactly!" Nathan tapped his nose and winked.

"Sorry, that action doesn't translate very well."

"Don't worry about it. I'd forgotten we were out of the influence of the ALSID. Are you sure you'll be able to manage without the option of switching on an ALSID for the whole time we're here?"

"Absolutely. It's the least of my worries."

"Hey, you! Get out of here!" A gruff, voice barked, accompanied by a face-full of torchlight.

"I think you could be right there," Nathan gasped. "Run!"

CHAPTER 6

Nathan clambered up the clattering fence to a backdrop of shouts and fist-shakes. The lithe Kayleesh overtook him as they scrambled over the barbed peak. He felt the stab of sharp barbs, felt the blood run, but determination spurred him on. He jumped to the floor, landing next to the Augtopian and they scampered across the street and into the shadows. They paused momentarily for breath in a urine-stained underpass where a middle-aged homeless man and a scruffy German Shepherd were sleeping under an old blanket.

"This is not exactly the first place I had in mind to show you!" Nathan laughed, in spite of himself.

"That's OK. We're not here to sight-see, are we?"

"True." Nathan looked at the homeless man. It occurred to him that he had less money about his person than lay in the poor man's cup. "We'd better move on. I don't want that guard to catch us and question us. We're trying to help save his planet from imminent invasion. There's just no pleasing some people."

"Where are we going?" Kayleesh asked.

"To the psychiatric hospital. to visit my mum."

Schlomm and Hannond Putt were delivering the last consignment of meat goods of the day. They had been lying low since Hannond's recent, unscheduled period of incarceration on the prison planet of Porriduum. Hannond had escaped, with the help of Tom Bowler and his malefic brother, and he did not want a repeat trip to the reviled place.

Hannond had been exiled to Porriduum for the most heinous crime. Heinous, if you were a Radiakkan, for he had unwittingly destroyed a Radiakkan flag. He had been holidaying on the sunny shores of the nationalistic planet when the extreme heat of the planet's dual suns had set the small, hairy creature ablaze. The panic-stricken Hannond had awoken from his slumber and rolled in what he had hoped was the direction of the cooling waters' edge. The journey of the tumbling rotund Glorbian came to meet with what he had taken to be a beach towel. The towel was, however, in fact a stretch of material emblazoned with the Radiakkan international flag. Desecration of the item had resulted in the harsh penalty of deportation to Porriduum. The irony of the situation was that Hannond was the milder of the two Putt brothers. It was *Schlomm* who revelled in law-breaking and corruption. He was the real space pirate, with his plotting and calculated diabolical deeds. It was down to Schlomm's plotting that he was able to plan a rescue mission. Or *half* plan one. He succeeded in his mission to the impenetrable planet, but unfortunately, he also succeeded in losing his spaceship in a miss-judged bet. He had been tricked by a Strellion. And not for the first time. Fortune shone on the brothers however, in the form of Tom Bowler, and the three of them had eventually managed to escape.

The venture had left the brothers lacking a spaceship, so they had sold their meagre possessions and put a down payment on a new ship; The Cluock II. Schlomm insisted that they steal one of course, but Hannond explained that he never wanted to see another bowl of Porriduum Porridge again. So here they were, building the family business back up again, the honest way. They were back to selling burger meat and vats of milkshake to fast food outlets galaxy-wide. Hannond still felt as though he was looking over his shoulder, afraid that his absence on Porriduum was going to result in a longer sentence should they ever catch him. But Schlomm simply scoffed.

"You can stop worrying about your sentence," Schlomm boomed. He hopped up onto the squat flight chair and tapped at the controls of the Cluock II.

"I can?" Hannond adjusted the blue sash which served as the Glorbian's only garments and padded across the bridge to his own flight chair.

"I hear that the Radiakkans have got more interesting things to bother themselves with than your petty crime these days."

"They didn't think it was so petty."

"True, but if you were going to get sent to Porriduum at least make it worth-while."

"Can we not go through this again?" Hannond sighed. "Tell me Schlomm – what are the Radiakkans busying themselves with that's so important?"

"I hear that they're invading a planet. A planet of humans."

"You want to visit your mum? At a time like this?" Kayleesh asked, walking quickly to keep up with her human friend. It is true that the first thing that a young male human thinks about, when catastrophe strikes, is how much they want their mum. Nathan was no exception.

"A time like this is the exact reason I want to visit her. Besides, I've not visited her in a while, and I need to check that she's OK."

"Well I supposed if it were me, I'd do the same." Kayleesh looked up at the still, dark sky and shivered. She pulled her hat down over her ears.

"We're miles away from home and I have no money for a train. So, it makes sense that we walk the few streets to the psychiatric hospital."

"OK, you don't have to justify it, Nathan. We'll go and see your mother. It's fine, honestly."

The pair walked through the city streets, the chilly evening air enveloping them. Nathan noticed that his alien friend had not aroused any suspicion thus far. People were too busy getting to where they needed to go to notice them, jumping onto buses, marching swiftly past or sauntering along in rowdy groups. He breathed in warm, spicy air, as they passed an Indian restaurant. He smiled at the thought of a proper Midland curry. How he wished he had some money in his pockets.

Suddenly Nathan shot out his arm, causing Kayleesh to almost topple over it.

"Nathan, wha -" she gasped and stopped suddenly. For, a young man who had staggered out of a pub was emptying the contents of his stomach onto the pavement in front of them. "Oh!" She exclaimed. "That's... that's..."

"...That's *not* what we wanted to see. Still, it's made me lose my appetite!" He steered her around the unfortunate gent and continued along the road.

"Why was he doing that?" Kayleesh screeched.

"It's not an uncommon sight in the city," Nathan explained. "I've been there myself once or twice."

"Oh, I remember when Tom was sick. He vomited all over that bully Baff Bulken in the lift. He said it was because he was so terrified. But I think it was an act of bravery. He certainly left Tom alone after that!"

"That must have been before I arrived. I forget how long you've known him."

"I miss him."

"Me too."

Nathan side-stepped another pavement pizza. He grimaced. His longing for Indian cuisine had certainly diminished. He felt light raindrops catching his hand as he walked. Then one on his head. Two, three, four, five, until soon heavy precipitation was pouring relentlessly onto them. Nathan hadn't experienced being outside in rain in so long that it actually delighted him. Kayleesh squealed and laughed and the two of them ran and splashed their way along the road like toddlers in new wellingtons. By the time they reached the psychiatric hospital, their clothes were saturated. Kayleesh wrung out her hat on the doorstep, raindrops hammering onto the porch roof above them. Water gushed from her hat and she hurriedly replaced it before they stepped inside. They wiped their sodden shoes on the mat and approached the reception desk.

"I'm here to see my mother," Nathan informed the receptionist, a middle-aged Asian man.

"I'm afraid visiting hours are over, sir."

"But I need to see her!" he protested. "I've not been for weeks and... well this could be my last chance!"

"I see," the receptionist sighed. "And who is your mother?"

"Carol Reed."

"Mrs. Reed?" The receptionist queried, in a manner which disquieted Nathan.

"Yes, yes. Is she all right?"

"Are you *Nathan* Reed?"

Nathan nodded.

"I'm concerned that neither your father nor yourself have responded to any of the hospital's correspondence."

"What are you talking about? What correspondence? I've not been at the house. I've er... been away."

"Mr. Reed, we've been writing and calling on almost a daily basis. Your mother seems to have had some sort of... episode."

"What do you mean? Can I see her?"

"We wouldn't normally allow it, Mr. Reed, at this hour. But under the circumstances then perhaps you should see her. You've been away you say?" The receptionist lifted a telephone receiver and made an internal call. "Paudy? Carol Reed's son is here... yes. Nathan... very well, I'll send him through." He turned to Nathan, sympathy evident in his eyes. "Doctor Byrne will meet you both on the other side of the double doors."

"Is she all right?" Kayleesh asked him.

"Doctor Byrne will explain everything, don't worry."

Kayleesh looked at Nathan, his brow as furrowed as hers. She forced a smile and took his arm.

They were greeted by the doctor, a stern-looking man with glasses. His skin was as white as his coat and his brow was damp with perspiration. Nathan thought that perhaps the doctor needed to take some medication of his own.

"What's wrong with my mother?" Nathan asked, as they followed Doctor Byrne into a lift. "Is she not recovering well from her breakdown?"

"Your mother's condition seems to have taken quite a turn," the doctor informed him. "We were seeing signs of improvement, but in the last fortnight there have been some strange... developments."

"What do you mean? And this place looks different somehow," Nathan observed as they stepped out of the lift. A shiver ran down his spine. And what had happened to his father? Why hadn't he made himself available and visited? Or at least responded to calls and letters from the hospital?

"Different?" Doctor Byrne asked.

"Where are all the patients?" Normally there were one or two people around that said hello to Nathan and his Dad.

"Why, they're in their rooms. It is very late."

"I... I suppose so." Nathan realised that his body clock had not yet adjusted. He didn't recognise Doctor Byrne from his previous visit. However, he had not before visited at this hour. But something seemed wrong here. Very wrong. He felt Kayleesh shivering, as she held his arm. Her long, soggy mane of hair and wet clothing made her look further discomfited. He regretted bringing her to such an undesirable place.

"Here we are, room fourteen."

"I remember," said Nathan.

The doctor allowed them into the room and followed them inside. The room appeared comfortable enough; just how Nathan remembered it. A bed lay against one wall, a wardrobe and chest of drawers on another. A cork noticeboard above a dressing table presented photographs of Nathan, his father Robert and mother Carol as a younger woman pictured with her siblings. The dressing table itself was host to an array of vanity items and knick-knacks, all perfectly positioned as though about to undergo inspection. Bottled nail varnish lined up in colour order from Purple to mauve, turquoise, orange and red. Even discarded tissues were neatly folded and placed neatly in a waste-paper basket. This was not unusual though. This is how Nathan remembered his mother, never a hair out of place. However, the middle-aged woman seated at the window was not immediately recognisable as his mother.

"Carol, I have someone here to see you," the doctor said. Carol did not turn around. Nathan took the empty seat beside her and followed her gaze. She was looking out at the night sky. The lilac curtains were pulled back as far as they would go, and a small ventilation window was open. Nathan knew that the window was opened at its maximum due to the hospital's safeguarding regulations.

"There are more of them here now," Carol's voice was soft and child-like. Gone was the authoritative tone of a woman in control of every aspect of her life, a woman always on the go. "I just saw another one. It was only a small one this time, but it was flying towards the city. Just a few streets away I should imagine. There are more of them. More visitors."

Nathan and Kayleesh looked at each other.

"Come now, Mrs. Reed. I've told you that you've been imagining these things, it's part of your condition. Now come away from the window and speak to your real visitors."

"Nathan!" Carol finally unglued her gaze from the window. Her large green eyes, once so sprightly, met with her son's. They flickered over to the pretty pale girl, a smile unconsciously flirted with her lips, then she looked back at Nathan.

"Mum, this is Kayleesh, a friend of mine and Tom's. Tom's girlfriend, in fact."

"It's so nice to see you, Nathan. Hello, Kayleesh, what a pretty name. Didn't Tom come along with you both?"

"He's on his way," Nathan said softly.

"Of course he is. He wouldn't want to let you out of his sight for long. Such a pretty thing."

Kayleesh smiled, a little embarrassed.

"Carol, have you taken your medication this evening?" Doctor Byrne interrupted.

"Yes, yes of course I have." Carol frowned. "The nurse dispensed it only an hour ago."

"Good. That's good," he said. Doctor Byrne sat down on the purple quilted bed and turned to Carol's son and spoke at low volume. "Your mother has been talking about *visitors* for the last two weeks. In fact, she's talked about nothing else. At first the staff thought that she was referring to family and friends who come to the hospital, but we have come to think that she is in fact talking about *other worldly beings.*"

Nathan felt Kayleesh's gaze. He tried not to react to the condescending tone of the doctor. He tried to remain calm and simply raised an eyebrow.

"Other worldly beings?" he repeated. "You mean, *aliens?*"

"Just go ahead and ask her," the Doctor offered.

Nathan gulped.

"Mum, is what the doctor tells me correct? Have you *seen* these visitors? These *aliens?*"

"Yes. You believe me, don't you Nathan? Where is Tom? I wish he was here. *He'd* understand."

"Who is this *Tom?*" the Doctor enquired.

"My boyfriend, Tom Bowler," Kayleesh stated, a little irritated. "He's very intelligent."

A bleeping sound suddenly alerted the doctor who immediately shot to his feet. Checking his pager, Doctor Byrne made for door, coughed and announced, "I'll leave you kids to it. Emergency on floor three. I'll be back shortly."

Thankful for the opportunity of some privacy at last, Nathan leaned closer to his mother.

"It's all right, mum. I believe you."

"Do you really? Would you say that if I wasn't your mother?" Her eyes were wide, uncertain.

"Yes, we *both* believe you."

Carol looked out of the window once more, searching the rainy skies. Nathan took her hand.

"You said you saw something tonight – you saw something land?"

She turned to look at him once more.

"Yes, I saw it land. I hope they're not after me. It wasn't far away – they could be on their way into the city!"

"They're already here," Nathan said.

"What?" Carol withdrew her hand, drew her legs up to her chest, panic-stricken.

"Calm down, mum, it's OK. I didn't mean to alarm you. I'm sorry. What I *mean* is that I know that they're already here because... because it was *us*. Kayleesh and I. You saw us land and we came straight over here to-"

"Now *stop* it, Nathan. There's believing me and there's humouring me. And I think that what you're doing is-"

"No, it's true, mum."

"But you're not a *visitor*. You're my *boy!*"

"Yes, I know, just listen to me mum. We can prove it to you!" He nodded at the girl sitting next to him. Taking her cue, Kayleesh gingerly removed her damp, woolly hat and tucked her soggy golden locks behind her elfin ears. She blinked and leaned closer, so that Carol could see her violet eyes more clearly. Carol gasped.

"You... but you're... but you're not like one of *them*. You're different. But you're certainly not human. Are you?" Carol spluttered.

"No, I'm not human. I'm from a planet called Augtopia. My people are peaceful. Well, where my father is concerned, that's debatable," Kayleesh laughed, then stopped herself. "Carol, these other visitors, where have you seen them?"

"I've seen them in the grounds and I've heard them out in the corridors."

"In the hospital itself?" Nathan asked, stunned. Carol nodded.

"I can't remember how or why or even when, but I have this image in my mind which I can't quite shake. Vile bluish creatures, barking orders in a strange tongue. Intolerant, even cruel."

"Radiakkans," Nathan and Kayleesh chorused.

"Do you know about them?"

"Unfortunately." Nathan sighed. "Actually, it's why we came back to Earth. To help save the planet... from the Radiakkan invasion."

"And they think *I'm* delusional?" Carol spurted. "Crikey Nathan. Even if all of this madness is actually true and these creatures are spreading more than their bad temper, how do you propose to save the Earth? And can we back track a bit? *Came back to Earth?* I think you need to explain things to me. From the beginning."

Schlomm Putt manipulated the cuboctahedron-shaped console on the bridge of the Cluock II. He rotated the square screens, tapping at them with his stubby, grey fingers, determined to glean any information he could relating to the Radiakkan invasion.

"Why are you so interested in this invasion?" Hannond asked rather huffily, juggling the ship's controls by himself as they careered away from the planet Spetula Seven. "They're happening all the time. And this ship won't fly itself!"

"Which is why you're flying it, brother dear. I've piloted it alone many times. I'm sure that you're quite capable." Schlomm tapped on another of the device's screens and cast a deeper scan. "Radiakka Two... human planet... but which planet?"

"You still haven't answered my question – why the sudden interest? If they're invading a human planet at least we know that Glorb won't be endangered. We're safe."

"You've certainly developed an attitude since you were in Prison," Schlomm snapped. "Granted, we know Glorb is safe, for now, but I'd still like to know where they're heading... Aha!"

"Aha? How have you managed to access such classified information anyway, Schlomm?"

Schlomm rubbed his coarse hands together in apparent merriment. "I haven't. Yet. But the Radiakkans have just placed the largest order I've ever seen."

"Perfect - Let's feed the troops!"

"Perfect indeed."

Nathan and Kayleesh were enjoying breakfast at the family dining table. They were feasting on eggs and toast and supping large glasses of ruffleberry milkshake, swinging their legs like a pair of innocent infants. Sunlight was beaming in through the window, ambient country music sounded from the kitchen radio. The scene was saccharine sweet.

Suddenly.

A beam penetrated through the perfect scene.

A deafening crash.

A sickening scream.

Darkness.

Utter blackness.

Only the sound of the country music could be heard against the ringing in his ears, the crooning singer, blissfully unaware. The music seemed amplified in the stillness. The darkness soon began to falter, dusty daylight breaking through. A smoke-filled, ashen kitchen came slowly into view. Debris littered the kitchen, dust and residue intruding on every surface. And where his friends had been sitting so innocently only moments beforehand, lay two small heaps of black sand. He screamed. And then the sickening sound of crunching metal, twisting and grinding, reverberated through the window. Something was coming towards the house. Something was coming for *him*. He closed his eyes and screamed again.

Tom Bowler awoke suddenly. His sheets damp with sweat and his heart pounding. Had he screamed out loud? His mind trying to make sense of reality once more, he got to his feet and found that the other bunks had already been vacated. It had been another vivid dream. His heart was filled with relief.

But as Tom showered in the sanitation cubicle, Tom knew that his anxiety was not totally unwarranted. His friends were potentially in imminent danger. Anything could be happening to them. His beautiful Kayleesh. He took his time, allowing the warm droplets to cleanse and soothe his skin, massage his back. By the time he had towel-dried his hair and pulled on his compsuit, Tom was thinking more clearly again. The panic had subsided, and logic had returned, wearing its sensible brown suit and prim glasses and putting his thoughts into order. He told himself that if he was to persist with these regular psychological states then his first stop on Earth would be the Psychiatric hospital with Nathan's mother. He had to keep it together; for the sake of his friends. For the sake of the Earth.

He glanced out of the corridor window on route to joining his team-mates. He half-expected to have his view obscured by trees or buildings or anything recognisable as being Earthly. But he recognised nothing. In fact, the sky was pink. And there were three moons.

CHAPTER 7

"I don't believe this!" Tom growled and marched down the corridor. He felt as though there was a boiler in his chest which was on the edge of exploding. He glanced around the mess hall, shaking with anger. Where was Ghy? Mayty Reeston wondered past him, sipping a hot beverage.

"Morning, Tom."

Tom decided to forgo the pleasantries. "Where's Ghy? Why aren't we on Earth? What's happening, Mayty?" he barked.

"I can answer all of those questions with one simple answer; emergency landing on Ronnus."

"Emergency landing? Why? What's going on?"

"Because of the crash with the asteroid belt. The crew need to make some emergency repairs."

"Crash? What crash?"

"Are you trying to tell me that you slept through it, Tom?"

"Apparently so. When was this? What happened?"

Mayty explained that the ship had collided with space debris several hours beforehand and that he had fallen from his bunk during impact. He rubbed his behind for emphasis. He went on to say that there had been a great deal of noise and smoke and the strike had resulted in damage to the ship. Tom supposed that the commotion had broken into his dreams and fuelled his nightmares.

"Miraculously, there was barely a bruise amongst us. I'm sorry that no one woke you. I assumed that the crash would have got everyone out of their beds. The noise must have been ten times louder than the TSS alarm! Except when I was rudely awoken, I was relieved that it *wasn't* the TSS alarm waking me up for work."

"You were relieved that you were involved in a crash instead?" Tom laughed. "And that you'd fallen out of bed and hurt your bum?"

"Well not exactly, when you put it like that..." Mayty chuckled. "If the rest of the human race is half as funny as you, Tom, they're definitely worth saving."

"So how bad is the damage to the ship?" Tom braced himself for the answer.

"According to Ghy, the diagnostic report reeled off a number of issues; all minor enough for us to have been able to safely reach the nearest habitable planet. It's not really my field of expertise, to be honest."

"I thought that this would be up your street – after all, you're the one with all the maintenance skills."

"There's a galaxy of difference between unblocking a ruffleberry milkshake mixer and patching up a spaceship, Tom. If you still want to find Ghy he's assisting Chazner, Ranser and the engineering crew with repairs. Otherwise, Raphyl, Gracer Menille and her brood are out exploring, I believe."

"Well, my area of expertise doesn't cover spacecraft repair either. I think I'll go and find Raphyl and Gracer. Are you coming?"

"You carry on, Tom. I'm going to go and re-cooperate from my fall in one of the Ronnus' brine lakes; less pressure on the old backside." He winked and rubbed at his behind once more. "You should be able to catch up with them if you hurry, they only just left. Head in the direction of the hills. They've taken an ALSID bot with them."

Tom was surprised that Raphyl hadn't also chosen to take the opportunity to laze about on the salty waters of Ronnus' brine lakes; doing nothing was Raphyl's favourite sport. A few months ago, Tom would not have believed that he would find Raphyl clambering up hills when there were other options available to him. It was probably Gracer's influence. Or the absence of a bar. Or both. Raphyl certainly had a cheery demeanour about him in the presence of the Menilles. Tom spotted a cluster of people a hundred or so metres away. The beings were Raphyl and

Menille shaped and rapidly disappearing behind the next hill. He quickened his pace.

The ground was soft and carpeted in foliage - deep reds, purples and greens. The still lake lay to the east and three pale moons reflected in the cool waters, with remarkable effect. He breathed in the air. It really was a truly impressive sight. Kayleesh would have loved such a breath-taking view. Tom wondered whether Ronnus offered honeymoon packages. He grinned to himself.

The lower gravity of the planet allowed Tom to reach his friends at a faster pace than he had expected. Raphyl also seemed to have a spring in his step, as Tom discovered him galloping alongside Gracer and her lively hatchlings, although Tom suspected that his energy had little to do with low gravity.

"Oh, you're alive, then Tombo?" Raphyl said, walking backwards and pointing at him. He didn't seem too disappointed that he had interrupted his moonlit walk with the Menilles.

"Looks like it," said Tom. The ALSID bot had evidently already been programmed to accept English in advance of his arrival.

"Tom!" He was suddenly surrounded by the juveniles, who seemed to have aged again during the night. They certainly appeared almost as mature as their mother now. "Are you all right?" They chorused. And then a bombardment of questions:

"Did you hear the crash?"

"Did it wake you?"

"Did you know what happened to the ship?"

"Girls, girls..." Gracer admonished. "Stop hassling him. Calm down all of you."

"Yes, I'm fine," grinned Tom. "It didn't wake me, no, but I heard what happened."

"Aren't you angry that we're being delayed further?" Gracer asked, concern in her voice. "We're still no nearer to Earth."

"I *was* angry. But where is being angry going to get me? We're here and there's nothing I can do about it, apart from get in the way while they try to fix the ship. At least we survived the crash. We may as well make the best of it."

"That's right, Tombo," said Raphyl. "Great philosophy."

"Have you ever met the natives of Ronnus, Raphyl?"

"Nope."

"Me neither," Tom said.

"I guessed that," Gracer giggled.

"Hey, I'm quite well travelled now, you know," Tom said, hurt. "How do you know that I haven't served a burger to a native of Ronnus? Or that I haven't met any on Porriduum?"

"Oh, you won't have. The people of Ronnus are... a little... backwards. In their experiences of other worlds and cultures I mean."

"Like humans!" Raphyl guffawed.

Gracer laughed. Her children giggled.

"Why does it feel like you're all ganging up on me?" Tom gave a mock pout.

"You'll see what I mean," said Gracer. "Let me put it this way - we had to bring our own ALSID bot, didn't we? Which is not entirely unusual, but even the public places won't accommodate for multi-lingual conversations. The only reason no one has rushed to see why a spaceship has landed on their planet is because they're not expecting it to happen. No one here knows what a spaceship is.

"Well that's where humans are different. Most of them *know* what a spaceship is - even if they've never seen one. Give us *some* credit – we got to the moon."

"Your *own* moon," Raphyl pointed out.

"True, we are a bit behind, but given time..."

"See," Raphyl said. "Backwards."

Carol Reed seemed to be digesting the information that her son and the alien girl had given her. She had looked perplexed at first, but now her face showed signs of relief; she wasn't insane after all.

"So, *all this time,* Tom Bowler has been on living *on another planet serving burgers* at an *alien service station.* But... what about Exeter?"

"He never *went* to Exeter. That was just what he told his parents," Nathan said.

"And you… you were *abducted* from our back garden and taken to the very same planet, by the *Greys* who are actually... now let me get this right... inter-galactic policemen?"

"That's right."

"And now you're back to save the day?"

"Well that was the idea. But we don't know where to start," said Nathan.

"Inform the police! The army!" Carol stood up, gesticulating dramatically.

"And end up on in here with you, powerless to do anything?" Nathan frowned. "I don't think it'll help. But you might be able to help us – tell me more about the blue creatures. How long have they been here and why? What else have you seen?"

"I've told you all I know." Carol shook her head, forlorn. "And I'm experiencing problems with distinguishing fact from fantasy. I've been told I'm delusional for so long and been prescribed with so many pills that it's hard to determine what's real anymore. It's that doctor. He… he's unusual in his practices."

"Doctor Byrne?" asked Kayleesh.

"No, not Doctor Byrne. He's quite normal. Most of the time. Doctor Lomah."

"Another new Doctor?"

"I'm not sure how new he is… I… forget…" Carol slumped back down onto her seat, riddled with confusion.

"What is it that's so unusual about him? Is he one of the Radiakkans?"

"I don't think so… I'm not sure… he just seems… different."

"Alien?"

"Perhaps." Carol looked about her in puzzlement. "There was a glass of water somewhere."

"Here," Kayleesh handed her a half full beaker which had been sitting on top of a chest of drawers.

"Thank you, sweet-heart," Carol said and shakily took a large gulp before cradling the container in her hands. "I'm due to see the doctor again tomorrow. After lunch. I'll concentrate and take note of what he says, of what he looks like, and report back to you."

"I wish there was a way that we could go with you," Nathan sighed. "Surely they can't stop me being there?"

The bedroom door suddenly opened. Doctor Byrne entered and walked swiftly over to window.

"Is it over?" Kayleesh asked the doctor.

"Is what over?"

"The emergency on floor three."

"The what? Oh... nothing to worry about, false alarm."

"That's good news," Carol smiled weakly and sipped her water.

"Really?" Kayleesh probed. She looked at Nathan.

"Yes..." The doctor stared out of the window, somewhat distracted. It was as though his mind was as distant as the stars on which his gaze was so transfixed. "Yes... everything... everything is just fine." Doctor Byrne turned to Nathan and Kayleesh. His mouth was set in a wide smile, but his eyes betrayed him. He looked almost maniacal for a second, as he looked from one to the other, then back again. His gaze finally fell on Carol and he seemed to normalise. "So, have you enjoyed having visitors today?"

"I… I… we were wondering, doctor, whether it would be all right if my son and his friend came with me to my consultation with Doctor Lomah tomorrow."

"Certainly not!" He stepped back. His body tense, he glared down at his patient.

"Why not?" Kayleesh asked. She wasn't scared of this man.

"Because it's not the practice of this establishment. What occurs in the consultation room is private. Have you not heard of doctor/patient confidentiality?"

"Well what if I agree to it?" Carol suggested.

"It's not a matter of you agreeing to it. How is the doctor supposed to do his job correctly and to a professional standard if he is being distracted? I will refer you to the Procedures if needs be; all of which Mr. Reed has signed on your behalf. How is the Doctor supposed to successfully carry out an accurate assessment with other people around?"

"Assessment? I thought that my mum was already being treated," Nathan asked.

"Yes, a period of treatment throughout which she is being continually assessed. You are welcome to visit her afterwards of course, during *authorised* visiting hours – this is a one off you understand – but your presence during that allotted time with the specialists is prohibited."

"I don't suppose we can argue with that," Carol whispered.

"Perhaps Dad didn't know what he was signing," Nathan protested.

Carol gave him a pleading look which suggested that she was tired of the conflict.

"All right," Nathan sighed. "Then, Doctor Byrne, may we meet with Doctor Lomah separately?"

"Separately, you say? Yes... yes... that could be arranged."

Nathan and Kayleesh stayed in the hospital's guest bedroom that night. For a nominal fee, friends and relatives of patients were allowed to stay in the twin room on occasion. They had not booked in advance of course, which was the usual practice of the establishment, but nothing about their visit was usual. Carol had willingly agreed to fund their stay.

They joined Carol and the other patients in the dining room early the following morning and broke their fast with scrambled eggs on toast and orange juice. Carol seemed a little brighter and fresh-faced that morning and had made the effort to style her hair and apply mascara and lip gloss. Nathan recognised a few of the other patients from previous visits, and everything seemed to be in place. However, he knew that all was not well here. He had not yet spotted any Radiakkans. Where were they hiding? Were some of them residing in the hospital or did they just visit to consult with the doctors? What was their interest in the hospital?

"Is everything all right with your breakfast?" Doctor Byrne had appeared at the table.

"Yes, fine thank you." Nathan was torn away from his thoughts.

"Can my staff offer either of you a glass of water? Or a hot cup of tea?"

Nathan politely refused and Kayleesh shook her head as she sipped her orange juice.

Doctor Byrne smiled curtly and swished over to another table.

"I can't get enough of the stuff!" Carol exclaimed and took a sip from her second cup that morning. "I would have thought that one of the first things you'd have wanted to do when you got back to Earth was to have a nice cup of tea!"

"It wasn't really a priority," Nathan said. "And mum *please* keep your voice down. No more talk of us being *back on Earth* or anything that may draw attention."

Carol simply took another sip of tea and shrugged.

"So, when do you think we're going to get the opportunity to meet Doctor Lomah?" Kayleesh asked.

"Doctor Lomah is in fact free now." Doctor Byrne spun around. He had evidently been listening in.

"He will have finished his breakfast by now and has an hour or so before his first consultation. So, young woman, would you like to go and see him first?"

"On my own?" Kayleesh asked. "Can't we go in together?" She looked at Nathan.

"The agreement was that you went in to meet with him *separately.*"

"Well it seems rather odd, but, if it's the only way..."

"It's the *only* way," he nodded. Nathan was beginning to understand what his mother had meant about the doctor's behaviour. He had seemed approachable and normal enough to begin with. But now he couldn't quite figure him out. He decided that it would be best to comply for now. "This way please," Doctor Byrne gestured towards a door at the far end of the dining room. Kayleesh chewed at her lip and looked at Carol and then Nathan. She scraped back her chair and stood up.

"I'll see you when you come out," Nathan said. "Don't worry."

"Why should she worry?" The doctor gave a little laugh and Kayleesh followed him out of the room.

Nathan looked at his mother whose brow was as furrowed as a recently ploughed field.

Tom Bowler finally understood what Raphyl and Gracer had meant about the people of Ronnus. They were very much like humans. In fact, they looked more like humans than Tom did. They were better groomed and walked with a proud Britishness that even the British did not possess, with walking sticks, top hats and obedient pets at their heels. As the motley bunch approached what appeared to be a small village, men and women walked stiffly through the streets and children played in the lane. The apparel of the inhabitants gave the impression of Sunday best. It was as though Tom had travelled back in time to Victorian England. A rural, Victorian England.

"This is so strange," Tom noted. "I feel almost at home, yet... so out of place."

"You fit in all right," Raphyl laughed. "You are just as strange as they are."

"We'd better not act too conspicuously," Gracer whispered. But it was too late for her children had already taken it upon themselves to embark on a game of catch with a group of local children. "And I thought that they had almost peaked at adulthood. Never mind. I'm sure it won't be long." She pushed a stray lock of her burnt orange hair out of her vision and observed the hatchlings. Tom looked on also. Wouldn't the well-dressed citizens notice that the six identical girls, who not only towered over them at six feet tall and wore strange clothes, but sported two sets of gills?

"I thought that the people here didn't understand outsiders," Tom said.

"Children are always accepting," said Gracer, simply.

Tom thought that perhaps this race wasn't so similar to humans after all; he had been bullied for much less.

"So, I'm assuming that this village has some sort of inn," Raphyl grinned.

"It's very unlikely Raphyl," Gracer giggled. "They haven't invented them yet."

"What?" Raphyl almost exploded. "I knew this planet was backwards but... *really?*"

"And there won't be any spotoon boards, which is probably why this was an unscheduled stop."

"So, if the people here don't even know anything of other worlds, then how do you know of them?" asked Tom.

"The same reason that your world doesn't know about us I expect. Ignorance," Gracer shrugged.

"Now look..."

"I'm sorry. I'm not being offensive, just truthful."

Tom was about to protest when a flurry of men ran past him, almost knocking him over.

Indigo-skinned men.

"Well?" Carol asked Kayleesh, who was sitting on her bed. "What did you think of Doctor Lomah?"

"It's hard to explain, really," admitted the Augtopian. She brushed a stray golden lock behind an elfin ear. Her violet eyes were deep in concentration. She looked up at Carol, who was seated on her window seat and leaning towards her, expectantly. "I can't quite puzzle it out. Meeting Doctor Lomah. It was as though..."

"Go on."

"I think I'll have to confer with Nathan, because if what I've just experienced is real... then we could be in a lot of trouble. I have to find out how Nathan perceived his meeting."

"How he perceived it? What do you mean? What did you experience, Kayleesh?"

"I... I... with every passing moment, I forget. It's as though my memory of it is... fading away."

"That's what happens to me!" Carol gasped. "I just know that there's something wrong about those consultations, and when I come out I always want to do something about it, but by the time I've got back to my room I've almost forgotten. And by then my medication has normally started to take effect and within a matter of minutes I'm asleep. You didn't... *take* anything did you?"

"No... no… I wasn't offered anything."

The two sat awhile, waiting for Nathan's return.

Kayleesh rushed over to the door the moment that the door handle turned. She beckoned him in before promptly shutting the door.

"Quickly, before you forget," she said. "What happened?"

"Hang on a moment."

"Before your memory fades. Come on, Nathan. It's important that you verbalise your initial thoughts!"

"Burgers!"

"What?" Kayleesh hissed, utterly dismayed. She flopped onto
the bed.

"Are you all right?" Carol asked.

"I'm perfectly all right... or at least I was. My thoughts are becoming muddled, but I keep thinking of *burgers...*"

"No… no... we need you to remember what happened in the consultation room." Kayleesh shook her head.

"That's what I'm doing," Nathan reassured her. He sat beside her and rested a hand on her shoulder.

"I saw how puzzled you looked on your way back up here and I told myself that I must try and retain as much information from the meeting as possible. Well I don't remember any of the actual conversation with Doctor Lomah, but the main impression which stuck was *burgers...* the notion of the Express Cuisine and an image of Raphyl working hard."

"Raphyl working hard?" Kayleesh almost laughed. Then she gasped. "Oh! You mean Miss. Lolah! Of course!"

"Will someone please explain to me what this nonsense is all about?" said Carol.

"Miss Lolah is a pherobot." Nathan explained the concept of the Express Cuisine's android supervisor to his mother. "And once you're out of the android's field of pheromonal influence, it's quite hard to imagine what it was like once you were in it. Does that make sense?"

"I... think so," said Carol.

"It's the same with the service station's prison guards. They use pherobots to control the inmates, to make them compliant."

"I'm not sure whether that's an ingenious or loathsome idea," Carol admitted.

"Well, it works," Kayleesh shrugged. "TSS have used them for generations. And I think that your Doctor Lomah is some kind of cousin of the pherobot. It seems to have an effect on all sexes, and it is being used to confuse and control. Much like the pherobots."

"Which the people of Earth are certainly not used to," Nathan added. "It would certainly explain a lot. I can't even remember what she looked like. But I suppose she *must* have looked like an android."

"I can't remember what he looked like either," Kayleesh gasped.

"What are they doing here?" Carol asked.

"I'm not sure. Who knows how many have been brought to Earth and where they've all been stationed?" Nathan shuddered at the thought.

"And what are the Radiakkans using them for? Why do they need them?" pondered Kayleesh.

"Precisely. What's our next move?" Nathan asked. Then said, "Mum, we need to get you out of here."

"No fear – I'm not going out there where the land is being invaded by aliens. I'd rather stay here and take my chances with the one android thank you very much. At least it's safe. But I worry for your father. I've not heard from him"

"I'm not so sure how safe it is here," said Nathan. "But I suppose if we do try and get you out of here, it would arouse suspicion."

"This is an impossible situation," Kayleesh sighed.

"Don't deliberate on my fate," Carol said, bravely. "Go and do what you've got to do. You have more of an idea what you're up against now."

"I'm not sure that we do. We don't know how big this is."

"I think that it's safe to assume that it's pretty big, Nathan," said Kayleesh.

"Oh dear." Carol suddenly got to her feet and ran into her small bathroom. They heard much retching and toilet flushing.

"Mum, are you all right?" Nathan hollered.

With sodden brow and ruddy cheeks, she eventually emerged. She took a long gulp of water and wiped her face with one of the tissues from the neat pile on her dressing table.

"It happens every now and then. More frequently these days, however."

"Why didn't you say anything before?" Nathan asked, a little crossly. "If you're ill..."

"If I'm ill then I'm in the right place. I'm no use out there. Now don't worry about me."

"But..."

"Look." Carol pulled open the bottom draw of the chest. She located a red leather designer purse and promptly disclosed a wad of notes. "Take this. I don't need it while I'm in here. Take the train. Find your Dad. Find out what's going on. Do what you came to do."

Nathan opened his mouth to object but knew that his mother would only implore that he took the money. They had no choice. Sitting with his mother, whether she was ill or not, was not going to help them progress. He took the cash and stowed it in his pocket before giving Carol a big squeeze.

Schlomm and Hannond Putt had a full cargo bay. A very full cargo bay. It was positively brimming. But not with burger meat. This time their hold was booming with gallon upon gallon of water. There were barrels in the corridor and barrels on the bridge. One of them had rolled over onto its side and almost mown down poor Hannond. He sat grumpily in his flight chair, eyeing the offending barrel with contempt.

"This is most unorthodox," Hannond grumbled. "I'm sure we've bypassed every single Glorbian health and safety law."

"*Health and safety law? On Glorb?*" Schlomm scoffed. "I think that you've been away from our home world far too long. That statement was rather oxymoronic."

"Well there *should* be some kind of law. Perhaps that's my next role. Health and safety officer. Who needs this amount of water anyway?"

"The Radiakkans have ordered it. You know that, my foolish brother."

"I was under the impression that they were ordering something to sustain the troops, good old-fashioned protein. What will they do with all of this? If they're invading a planet then I would have thought they'd invade a planet that had fresh supply of water already. Unless they were terraforming... which would take considerably longer."

"Maybe it's not for them," Schlomm shrugged. "Maybe it's not even water."

"Well if it's Glorbian Whiskey then I might be interested in attacking the barrel which almost flattened me into a Luenian splancake.

"It's unlikely, seeing as we just collected the consignment from the other side of Triangulum."

"Well I'm going to open one anyway," Hannond huffed.

The journey from city-centre to suburbia via train was familiar to Nathan. The carriages were quiet, with commuters going about their daily lives at their respective places of employment as though the world was a perfectly safe place to be. A mother rocked a sleeping infant in her arms while an older child happily licked sherbet from a lolly pop on the adjacent seat. An elderly couple shared a magazine, chuckling together at a story within its pages. The ticket collector sauntered through to the next carriage; all completely oblivious. Nathan leaned towards Kayleesh.

"Everything seems so normal." he whispered.

"This vehicle is normal is it?" Kayleesh raised an eyebrow.

"It's very ordinary, yes. But look around us. No panic. Everything is... normal. Just like in the psychiatric hospital."

"Well so it seemed. Until we found out otherwise," Kayleesh pointed out. "Maybe there's a pherobot driving this thing. Or a Radiakkan on the roof."

"As crazy as that sounds, you could be right. We have to be totally aware of any possibility. Particularly if they have the potential to mess with our minds and make us forget things. What if the Radiakkans have stronger pherobots in their artillery?" He looked about the carriage. "Maybe everyone on this train has seen one, but they've now forgotten."

Kayleesh looked at him, chewing on her lip, nervously. "But then how is it that we still remember?"

"Maybe it's because we already know of the existence of pherobots. If we'd never encountered one, then we wouldn't have noticed. Like my mother. She has met Doctor Lomah many times but had no idea that she wasn't human."

"True. I think there's more to it though, Nathan. I think there's something that we're missing."

The train drew to a stop and the pair jumped down onto the platform. A short taxi journey took them to the street where Nathan lived. Kayleesh looked about her, soaking in the environment.

"I can see the appeal."

"Of what?"

"Earth. I can understand why it would be chosen as a candidate for Radiakka II."

Nathan looked at her in horror. Why was she saying that? Had Kayleesh learned English correctly?

"I just meant that it's beautiful. I'm not going to encourage my race to invade or anything!"

Nathan said nothing. He realised that he was being over-sensitive. It felt strange to be standing on his doorstep once more after so much had happened. He unthinkingly felt his pockets for something key-shaped and was surprised when the front door swung open to Kayleesh's touch.

"Now that *isn't* normal," he said. Cautiously he ventured inside, pushing past her. "Dad?" he called out. The hallway was dark, and the curtains were drawn. He tripped over a pile of unopened post. He wrinkled his nose at the unsavoury scent his olfactory system was being bombarded with. "Wow, Dad. You managed to let things get *even worse?"*

"Where is your father?" Kayleesh whispered.

"I wish I knew. I must admit that I'm getting a little worried now."

"Your father is not here!" A voice barked from the gloom at the top of the stairs.

Nathan strained to see, but his eyes were met with darkness and dust.

A light flickered on and they were confronted with the speaker.

A tall, angry-looking Radiakkan descended the staircase.

CHAPTER 8

Nathan's grip on Kayleesh's hand tightened. The invader continued to approach them. With each descending step, Nathan's fear climbed.

"I suggest that you leave while you can," the Radiakkan barked.

"*I'm* not leaving – this is *my house*," Nathan managed. But he was trembling.

"How come we can understand you?" Kayleesh asked.

"Now is not the time to be worrying about things like that," hissed Nathan.

"Oh, she is a *clever* one." The creature was now on the bottom step. "We have already begun installing ALSIDs in the vicinity. We'd rather the expense of ten thousand of the devices than go to the trouble of learning your pitiful, *disgusting* little language."

"If you're so disgusted, why bother to communicate with Earth's inhabitants at all?" Kayleesh asked, bravely. In his bewilderment, Nathan wondered for a moment whether Kayleesh was now speaking in her own tongue or his.

"Oh, you'll soon see. And don't think that you're fooling anyone, *Augtopian*. That pathetic attempt of a disguise certainly doesn't deceive me."

"Leave her alone!" Nathan scowled at him. The Radiakkan had squared up to him. Nathan was flat against the door. He gulped.

"Oh, all right. I'll leave the entire planet alone while I'm at it, shall I? Call off the troops?"

The invader seemed to have a sense of humour. But Nathan wasn't laughing. His anger grew.

"Where is my father?"

"I told you. He's not at home. So, why don't you leave now and go back to wherever you came from?" His bulbous, blue nose was almost touching Nathan's.

"I am not leaving."

"We came here to save him. And we came to save the Earth," Kayleesh added.

The Radiakkan looked at her. Then he began to wheeze; gravely, laboured breaths. He stumbled away from Nathan, clutched at his stomach and tumbled back onto the bottom step of the staircase, utterly drained of energy.

He appeared to be *laughing*.

He was literally doubled over, gasping for breath between guffaws. The Radiakkan eventually found the strength to pull himself to a seated position, shook his head and gathered his breath.

"Well… whoever set up today's prank certainly got me," he said, finally. "For a moment I thought that these two characters were serious! Come out now, c*ome on*. Who sent these two prisoners in and how did you find such fine actors?" He got to his feet and looked about him, evidently expecting a third party. When no response met him, his indigo face slackened, and he turned back to the intruders.

"Don't tell me that… that you expect me to believe… Don't tell me that… that you two are being *genuine?*"

Nathan regretted that they had simply stood by and not attacked the creature while he was vulnerable in his state of mirth. He cursed himself for not attempting to at least restrain him. He knew exactly where in the house to find the apparatus that he would require. But it was too late. The Radiakkan was standing strong and resolute once more.

"Tell us what you're up to – how do you plan to take over the planet?" asked Nathan.

"And why should I tell you? Do you even know who I am?"

"You're an intruder in my house and on my home world!"

"I am Nigel, and I shall soon be Deputy Ruler of this land."

"Deputy Ruler of this land?" Kayleesh gasped.

"*Nigel?*" Nathan coughed. Kayleesh looked at him. "What? His name is more shocking than his title!"

"Why is it?"

"Because the idea that this creature could possibly be a ruler of England is simply not believable, but the idea of an invader being called *Nigel* is just... *absurd"*.

"*Believe it,* human." Nigel's eyes narrowed.

"If you're planning to be Deputy Ruler of England, or Earth, or however high your ambitions are, who is planning to be number one?" Kayleesh questioned him.

"That information is classified!" Nigel barked.

"Well that's not very good, is it? How are we going to know who to bow down to?" Nathan winked at Kayleesh.

"You won't need to know – because there won't be any of you left *to* kneel to the *Supreme Ruler.*"

"So, you plan to wipe out all of mankind?"

"We do." Nigel reached into his pocket and disclosed a dastardly looking device, which he promptly pointed at Nathan's head. "Starting with you two."

Dust scattered from the sandy road as Tom, Gracer and Raphyl scrambled out of the path of the indigo stampede and ducked behind a fence. Tom soon found himself shielded by a wall of Menilles.

"Was that -"

"Radiakkans!" Gracer gasped.

"What are they doing here?" Tom hissed.

"Radiakka III?" Raphyl suggested, casually.

"Don't say that!" one of Gracer's children whimpered.

"They wouldn't invade Ronnus. There are barely any resources. This is the only habitable continent," another daughter piped up.

"You're rather knowledgeable about this planet," noted Raphyl.

"I only know because we covered a module on this planet in school."

"Then tell us all you know," said Tom.

"I didn't say I passed the course."

All nine got to their feet and dusted themselves down. Tom peered down the pathway. There was no sign of the Radiakkans. The local children might have been complaisant and obliging in nature, but there was no sign of them now.

"Where did everyone go?" asked Tom.

"Perhaps they're all hiding, too," said Raphyl. "How about I go and ask inside this bar."

"I don't think that's a bar, Raphyl," one of the Menilles warned.

"It's worth a try..." his voice trailed off and Raphyl was already crossing the road.

Gracer and Tom looked at each other.

"I suppose we should follow him," Tom said.

Once inside, Tom was suddenly filled with a comforting sense of snugness which he could only associated with the nostalgia of the Christmases of yesteryear. The cosy interior boasted a roaring fire and the modest fireplace was embellished with foliage, twisted twigs and frosted berries. Two tattered armchairs faced the fire and a contented pet of some breed or another was dozing on the one closest to the fire. Tom found that the air was fragrant with spices and the warmth of the place enveloped him. A small desk on which rested a cashiers' till at the far end of the room seemed at odds with the rest of the scene. A well-dressed lady, as prim as she was proper, swished through an archway behind the desk and eyed the visitors. She patted her hair which was pinned up to perfection and adjusted her spectacles. Her fluid movements suggested a woman in her confident thirties, at least as far as Tom could judge, but the lines on her face were well etched. The overall image confused him, but he had learned not to stare. Gracer managed to programme the ALSID bot to respond to the local language, moments before the lady spoke.

"Are you all part of the carnival?" she asked. Her voice was light and pleasant.

"Carnival?" demanded Raphyl. "I just came in for a drink. I don't expect that you serve Truxxian Gloop, but I'm not feeling that fussy."

"Raphyl!" Gracer admonished him.

"Oh, yeah," said Raphyl. "We were wondering where everyone went – when the Radiakkans ran past."

"The blue people – a whole herd of them – they ran past your er... establishment," said Tom.

"The younger generation aren't used to a carnival," said the woman behind the desk. She turned to Gracer. Her face cracked into a smile.

"My poor dear, would you like to try a free sample of my exclusive, locally sourced, wrinkle cream?"

"Don't you mean *anti*-wrinkle cream?" "*Anti*-wrinkle cream, dear? Why on Ronnus would anyone want such a product?" She ran a hand over her face, apparently delighting in its deep-set ridges and grooves. "I'm sorry, are you in costume?"

"No, this is my real face. We're not part of the carnival," Gracer informed her.

"I'm sorry to hear that dear, then you must try some wrinkle cream. Here, take a pot for free. I insist." Gracer took the pot out of politeness. "I can't promise any miracles, but the sooner you start using the cream, the sooner it'll work. It might not be too late to start helping the smaller ones," she said, indicating Gracer's children. Gracer forced a smile and pocketed the cream.

"How long has the carnival been in town?" Tom asked, desperately trying to get on the strange elderly lady's level. He wasn't even sure that she was elderly. On arrival, Ronnus had seemed the most Earth-like place that he had experienced in his travels. But things here were making less and less sense.

"The carnival has been here for a few weeks now. At first there were only a few of them; they gathered by the brine lakes. Then came more. But now they seem to be going again."

"They're leaving?" asked Tom.

"Yes, there have been fewer and fewer of them of late. They are strange creatures, always moving so swiftly about the place." Then she added, by way of some strange reasoning, "Maybe they're from the lost continent."

"Maybe. So where are they all going to?" Tom asked, confused.

"Back to the lost continent I assume. I don't know. I don't travel much. Do you have a lady friend? Perhaps you might like to take her a sample of my exclusive, locally sourced, wrinkle cream."

The door leading to the downstairs bathroom burst open. A balding, middle-aged man flopped onto the hallway carpet. He looked as though he had just escaped from a particularly unbearable sauna. But instead of a waft of heat, the open door released a waft of putrid stench. The man turned to the visitors. His eyes were bleary, and his beard was vomit sodden. Nathan's father stood up, wavering, faltering.

"Nathan?"

"Dad?"

Nigel's attention was momentarily side-tracked. Nathan quickly ducked out of the path of the alien device aimed at his head and Kayleesh took the opportunity to knee Nigel where she hoped his genitals would be. With a cry, Nigel re-joined his old friend, the bottom step, as he writhed in agony. Kayleesh grabbed the device from the Radiakkan's hand and introduced her boot to Nigel's face. It was taking them a while to get acquainted, so she had to introduce them several times.

Nigel soon lay unconscious.

"Good work, Kayleesh," said Nathan. "Dad, what happened?" He took his father's arm and manoeuvred the weak man into the lounge.

"Nathan, what are you doing here? What's happening? What was that blue thing?"

"I'll tell you later. I need to know what happened to *you* first, so we can help you. What were you doing in there for so long?"

"I've been sick, Nathan, so very sick. I must have passed out for a while. I had to get out of there it was so… just don't go in there!"

"I wasn't planning to!"
Robert relaxed into the chair. He looked a little calmer now and the redness in his cheeks was fading, the sweat on his brow, dissipating. Where was Kayleesh? Nathan called her.

"I'll be there in a krom," she called back.

"What are you doing?"

"Trying to find out what happened. Trying to find out why everyone on this planet is constantly being sick. Unless it's some kind of welcome tradition I wasn't aware of."

"No, no it's not. And you're right. The man outside the pub, my Mum and now Dad. There is definitely a pattern here."

"Not the prettiest pattern," Kayleesh appeared in the doorway, grimacing as she brushed some stray puke from her clothing.

"So, did you find anything? Apart from the last of my stomach bile?" Robert murmured.

"No, nothing that would seem significant."

"Have you eaten anything that's disagreed with you, something that you wouldn't normally eat?" Kayleesh asked.

"I haven't eaten a thing since I went to the football match at the weekend."

"And what did you have to eat there?"

"Just a bag of nachos. I didn't have anything to drink. I was driving because I had to drop Mad Dave, Tall Dave and Andy back in Cannock after the game."

"And what about Mum? Why haven't you responded to the hospital's calls?"

"I knew there was something important that I needed to do. I just kept… forgetting. And then I got ill."

"When did you last go and see your wife?" asked Kayleesh.

"I er… er… last week I think."

"But the receptionist told us that they'd not heard from you for a fortnight," Nathan said.

"He did? I don't know… I've been so confused lately. Nothing seems to have any order anymore. I was so certain

I knew what was real and what wasn't at one point. When did that all change? I don't remember."

"Mr. Reed," Kayleesh said softly. "When you last went to see Carol – it doesn't matter when that was – did you go in and speak to the doctor? Doctor Lomah?"

"Yes… yes… I remember a Doctor Lomah. Nice woman."

Kayleesh and Nathan looked at each other.

"And what did she say to you? Can you remember anything about your conversation with her?"

"She offered me a cup of tea," he said vaguely. "She offered me a cup of tea, we talked, and I shook her hand and I came home. Nice woman."

"Dad, do you want to go and have a lie down? I'll get you some water while you get yourself up to bed."

"Yes, that sounds like a good idea." He got up, with his son's help, and made his way out of the room.

"Wait a minute, I'd better go and remove the alien on the stairs first." *I never thought I'd ever hear myself say that,* thought Nathan.

"I'll fetch the glass of water," offered Kayleesh.

When Nathan returned to the hallway, Nigel was beginning to stir. Before he had time to regain his senses, Nathan gave the alien a swift kick to the head. He grabbed his clammy arms and dragged the creature through to the rancid downstairs bathroom. He took great pleasure in hauling him onto the toilet, which was dripping in vomit. The Radiakkan was slumped over his bony knees, like a slovenly drunkard. Confident that the creature would not be moving for the time being, Nathan ventured out to the garden shed to retrieve a length of rope and a sharp knife. On his return, he found Kayleesh standing guard, with the alien device pointing squarely at the slumbering creature. Nathan smiled in admiration and then proceeded to wind the rope around the Radiakkan, securing him to the toilet. He cut off a smaller length and bound Nigel's face.

"Why are you gagging him?" Kayleesh whispered. "How is he going to speak if you gag him?"

"Why would we want the wretched creature to speak?"

"Well how else are we going to interrogate him?"

"Is that what we're doing?" Nathan stared at the enemy, tied helplessly to the toilet bowl. Then he looked up at the alien wielding the gun at said enemy. "You're right," he said and tugged the prisoner free of the makeshift gag. "I wasn't thinking straight. It's been a long day."

Nigel murmured incoherently. Kayleesh reflexively changed her stance, looking markedly tense. The Radiakkan took a few moments to absorb his surroundings. He glared in disgust and struggled fruitlessly against the tight restraints. He saved his most disgusted glare for his captors, however.

"How dare you detain the Deputy Ruler of Earth?" he barked.

"The *Deputy Ruler of Earth* is looking rather pathetic at this moment. If you *are* to be ruler, maybe I should send a photograph of this esteemed little scene to the tabloids now – I am sure that I would make a few thousand pounds," Nathan laughed.

"What is this rubbish you talk about, photograph, tabloids, pounds? You really are a loathsome race with loathsome diction."

"What are you doing in Nathan's house?" Kayleesh interjected, in a business-like manner.

"I told you, it's no longer *Nathan's house. You,* dear child, are the invaders."

"Why this house?"

"Why not? I wanted to see how the hapless humans lived. This house seemed as good as any, until you two arrived." He wriggled more violently. "Get me off this seat right now!"

"Why are the people of Earth being sick? What have you done to them?"

"You can't keep me here, it's inradiakkan. What if I should need to excrete?"

"I've visited bathrooms on Wheyland. They're not so different. Therefore, I'm sure this *seat* is more than suitable for your needs."

"*You've been to Wheyland?*" he spat.

"Of course! Why is that so unusual? It seemed to be a popular tourist spot but I'm not sure why. It's a detestable place. The dragon flies are more desirable than you evil…"

"Will you please stop the senseless point-scoring?" Kayleesh interrupted once more. "This is getting us nowhere. Nigel, just answer the relevant questions!"

"Why should I, Augtopian?"

"Because I'm the one holding the gun."

"True, but you don't know how to use it."

"How do you know that I don't?" Kayleesh asked, none too convincingly.

"Whether she does, or she doesn't, I still have *this,*" Nathan exclaimed and brandished the knife which he had stowed behind the cistern. He detected a flinch from the prisoner.

"Why are the people of Earth being sick?" Kayleesh re-iterated.

"She doesn't give up, does she?" Nigel sighed.

"Never. Well?"

"The whole race is a disease on this planet. It's time they knew what that felt like."

"What do you mean by that?" Nathan asked.

"You're too emotionally involved in this planet. It might be best if I asked the questions," Kayleesh suggested. "I can be more objective. Feel free to brandish away with your weapon though." She winked at him.

Nathan grinned back at her. She was right. His anger was fuelled by seeing his family so ill at the hands of these invaders. He was finding it difficult to hold any proper perspective.

"It's time we took over the rule of this planet. The humans have had control for long enough. So, we're eradicating every single last one of them."

"How?"

"You've seen how. And, if I have anything to do with it, there will be other ways. Faster ways."

"Is there a cure to the sickness?"

"Why should there be a cure?"

"Well, what if you should catch the sickness?"

"We won't"

"How do you know that?"

"Because we've taken the precautionary measures."

What are the precautionary measures?"

"STOP THIS INTERROGATION AT ONCE!"

Nathan turned round slowly to face a weapon very much like the one that Kayleesh was wielding.

But it was twice the size.

And the Radiakkan that was in possession of it was the personification of fury.

CHAPTER 9

Tom Bowler turned the wrinkle cream pot over and over in his pocket. He knew that he should have discarded the ridiculous item, but it made him feel close to Kayleesh, somehow. It was not something she would have a use for, but it reminded him of her femininity. He wondered how Kayleesh was surviving on Earth. Was she fighting, plotting, hiding, being her usual rave self? He suspected that she would be doing something clever. He squeezed the pot tightly in his fist. How he hoped to be with her soon. And how he wished he had something of hers that he could treasure, a photograph or a trinket. He only had his memories.

That's what he'd do. He'd buy Kayleesh a gift and when he next saw her, he'd present it to her so that if they were ever apart again, she'd have something to remember *him* by. But what? Jewellery was too formal, and it might not hold the significance it did with couples on Earth. Clothes? They weren't very exciting and aside from the logistics of venturing half-way across the universe with an armful of pretty fabric, he didn't feel much like clothes shopping.

They were back out in the lane now and Gracer was kneeling down, filling the ALSID bot with glow rocks which had been stashed in her pocket.

"Gracer, while we're waiting for the ship to be fixed, we may as well look around, right?"

"Of course. Isn't that what we're doing, Tom?"

"Do you think we have time to do a bit of shopping? I'm hoping that other shop keepers on Ronnus aren't as crazy as the wrinkle cream woman, but I was thinking that perhaps I could take the opportunity to buy Kayleesh a little gift."

"His planet is in peril, but at least his girlfriend has a new pair of earrings, right Tombo?" Raphyl laughed.

"Don't listen to him," Gracer said. "I think that it's a lovely idea. We may as well, while we're here. What kind of gift did you have in mind?"

"Well that's what I wanted to ask you. What do girls from Augtopia like?"

"That's a bit specific, Tombo," sneered Raphyl. "What do girls like, full stop? No one knows!" Tom laughed and Gracer's expression made him laugh all the more. "What about a Radiakkan music card?"

"Not the best idea after last time!" Gracer scowled at him. "How about we just have a look around and if I see anything that I think she might like I'll advise you?"

"Good idea."

"So, are we just going to ignore the fact that there are dozens of Radiakkans running around and go *shopping?*" one of the Menilles asked. "Shouldn't we at least try and find out what's going on here?"

"You heard the mad old lady, the *carnival* is leaving town," her mother said, simply.

"Exactly, she's a mad old lady. What does *she* know?"

"Maybe she's right," Tom shrugged. "I mean, *what am I doing here?"*

"Come on, Tom. Stop worrying. If we see anything suspicious, I'm sure we can handle it." She grabbed Tom's arm as they trooped along the dusty path.

"Gracer," Tom whispered. "I know it might seem a bit late in the day, but the longer we go on, the more awkward it's going to be so... I may as well get it over with."

"That sounds ominous."

"What? No! Er… what I want to ask is… what are your children's names? I am starting to tell them apart by the way they speak and act, but it would probably be ignorant of me if I didn't at least *try* and learn all their names."

"Oh, I see," Gracer said. She giggled. "Marry."

"What?"

"Marry. That's the name of my offspring; Marry Menille."

"Which one?" Tom looked about him as the hatchlings criss-crossed across the lane in their child-like manner, skipping and giggling.

"All of them."

"They all have the same name?"

"No, silly. They're *all* Marry."

"I'm not sure I follow."

"I thought you knew."

"If I didn't know that you were about to lay an egg that day in the Wheylandian Parliamentary Building, how do you expect me to know anything about teenage Menilles?"

"You don't even know the name of our race, do you? I originate from Mescapar. Historically, Mescaparians lay clutches of eggs which hatch and disperse into the world. They gather as much life knowledge as they can, and each hatchling is slightly different from the rest, so that they handle and deal with each experience differently. The strongest traits are brought out in each hatchling and when they reach maturity, they will re-group and pool their experiences and wisdom in one offspring. These factions will eventually become my daughter."

Tom did not know what to say in response.

"Of course, this is what has happened *historically*, but I have not brought up my offspring on Mescapar. Hence, the hatchlings were not able to scatter throughout the land throughout their childhood. I wanted to keep them close to me on Radiakka, given the circumstance. The child will not be as worldly-wise as one brought up on my home world, but this is often the case these days. It's rather common. And she will have a stronger bond with me, her mother."

"Which means I don't have to worry about which one to choose," Raphyl said, suddenly taking Gracer's other arm.

"Well… we'll see about that," smiled Gracer.

"Wow," is all that Tom could muster. He looked up and watched Marry interact, laughing and running ahead of them. *So Raphyl wants to marry Marry Menille.* "So, when will this amalgamation take place? And how?"

"She is nearly ready for her infusion."

"When there is only one of them, won't you miss the other five?"

"How can I? They'll all be her. And I'm sure I've mentioned to you before that this is not my first batch. I have other offspring out there. This is my youngest and I intend to keep her close. At least until we're somewhere more settled."

Tom's jaw refused to re-engage with the rest of his skull for the next ten minutes as he tried to make sense of the revelation.

"I suppose it makes sense in a way. It is quicker than just one person experiencing things one at a time," Tom mused. "Although maybe you'd have more things to regret doing,"

"Or fewer things to regret *not* doing," Gracer added.

"But... one more question... I'm sorry for being morbid, but I'm intrigued to know what happens if one or more hatchling from a batch..."

"- dies?" Gracer interrupted him. "Then when they fuse, the adult Mescaparian is an Incomplete."

"An Incomplete? What does that mean?" Tom asked, and more questions came flooding out. "Is that dangerous? What are they like, the Incompletes??"

"Tom," Gracer sighed. "*I'm* an Incomplete."

"You are?" Tom gulped. "So that means... that you have experienced death?"

"No, because the experiences that that hatchling had, died with her."

"Of course. I'm sorry, it's just hard to get my head round."

"I suppose it must be. I can't imagine a childhood any other way, though. I remember exploring the outer villages of my country, meeting my first boyfriend in the city and hiking up the highest mountain range. I also remember investigating the oceans and living amongst the fishermen, which is where I met my other first boyfriend."

"This is all too confusing," said Raphyl. "I really need to find a bar."

"This place looks like it might be interesting," said Gracer, pointing to an old-fashioned looking boutique. Tom followed as did a reluctant Raphyl. The store's contents were indeed a source of fascination for the travellers, but Tom felt as lost as he had on that first trip to Harmonious Sounds, where he had bought his melody mech. But instead of being confounded by alien technology, he felt as though he were in a museum. He was presented with case after case of oddities where no two items were the same. An elderly man dozed behind an old, musty desk. At least, he appeared to be elderly. It was either customary to work well into retirement age on Ronnus, or this gentleman was a customer of the owner of the previous shop. Tom wiped some dust from the top of one of the cabinets. Underneath the dusty glass glistened a row of oddments, each encrusted with glittering jewels. He stepped away from the treasure and peered into the next cabinet, hoping to encounter something which would not cost him all of his limbs.

"Gracer," said Tom, trying to make out what the leathery novelties in the case were used for. "How am I going to pay for anything? I don't suppose they accept Ds here."

"I hadn't considered that," she replied.

Tom ran a hand through a rack of dangling strips of shimmering material. He thought that perhaps they were for decorative purposes, but when something sharp pierced his skin, he realised that some of them seemed to be concealing tiny tools. He moved away, in the hope that Gracer was having more luck.

"Kayleesh might like one of these," Gracer suggested. She pointed through the glass of one of the cabinets at a small, smooth, pot.

"Do you think so? It looks rather... well... dull."

"Oh, but it's made from paska. Paska rock can only be found on Ronnus."

"It sounds expensive then."

"Why should it be? The people of Ronnus know of no other worlds. Paska rock is not considered precious to them."

"Maybe." Tom shrugged.

Suddenly, like a whirlwind in a porcelain shop, in burst the gaggling brood of Menilles.

"Oh, oh it's the carnival!" The shopkeeper suddenly burst into life, as though someone had flicked a switch.

"We're not part of the carnival," Raphyl sighed. "Why does everyone keep insisting that we are?"

"Not you, the young ones!"

The Menilles calmed themselves and began to talk in hushed tones.

"Oh, don't stop on my account. Let the entertainment commence!" he clapped joyously and surprised Tom further by hoisting himself onto the counter in one move. He sat there, swinging his legs and calling, "the Carnival has come to Pappsie. Sing and dance and twirl for Pappsie My!"

"Well, go on Marry," Gracer urged. "You heard Mr My. Entertain the man!"

The girls looked at their mother and then at each other. They paired off and began their haphazard leap-frog dance routine. They started to chant;

"Ghy Hasprin is no has-been, he has the best team and they are mean."

"Marvellous!" the gent cried. "I have no idea what you're singing about but it's marvellous. Carry on!"

They chorused the same line twice more, until one of offspring stopped leaping about, stood facing the shop keeper, and sang;

"Pappsie My, is a fun guy, he has the best things we wish to buy."

"Delightful!"

"Do you get the impression that the further along this lane we go, the more insane the citizens of this town will get?" Raphyl whispered to Tom.

"If we go much further, I have the feeling we'll actually stumble upon an asylum."

"Perhaps we're already there, Tombo!" Raphyl crossed his eyes and raised his hands in a mock scary stance. "Perhaps we'll never escape!"

The two of them laughed.

The shop keeper gave the cheerleaders a standing ovation.

"You have cheered up Pappsie My today, on this, his very birthday." A wide smile crept across his face. "And for that, Pappsie My shall reward you, my friends. Take anything, anything you wish, from my humble emporium."

"But it's *your* birthday," said one of the girls.

"Exactly. And you've given me the gift of mirth. It is your turn to choose a gift from me."

"I think that we should let Tom choose," Gracer told them. "For Kayleesh. Is that all right, girls?"

Marry didn't appear to mind. The six of them were already engrossed in a game of tag and running back outside, into the lane.

"Thank you," said Tom. This was definitely turning out to be one of the top ten most absurd days of Tom's life. Tom chose the paska stone pot.

"Is that all?" the shop keeper looked confused. "You can have anything in my shop. Anything at all!"

Tom looked about the emporium, still unsure of the purpose of most of Pappsie My's wares.

"I could help you to decided," he said, opening the first cabinet Tom had browsed with a small, golden key. He held aloft one of the jewel-encrusted trinkets. "This will fit nicely inside that paska stone pot. What say you?"

"I say thank you very much!"

"No, thank *you!* Pappsie My will always remember the day the carnival visited him!"

Inside a once quiet, suburban semi-detached house in England, Earth, two heavily armed indigo-skinned alien creatures were escorting two pale-faced people out of the building by force. The third member of the troop was busy separating the future deputy leader of the planet from the seat of a rather filthy toilet.

"*Dad!*" Nathan called out as he struggled against the burly arms of his captors. But his shouts met with silence.

Once out in the street, both Augtopian and human screamed until their lungs flattened.

"Scream again and you will both lose your heads!" one of the Radiakkans hissed. Weapons were pushed hard against their heads. Where were all of the neighbours? Was his father all right? Before Nathan had time to think, he found himself being bundled into a vehicle.

It was an *ice-cream van.*

Can aliens drive ice-cream vans? he wondered.

Kayleesh was bundled in after him. The armed Radiakkans pushed Nathan and Kayleesh to the floor. They joined them on the cramped floorspace. Nathan heard Nigel's voice, and the sound of both doors slamming shut. As the engine rumbled into life and the vehicle began to move, the ice cream van chimed a loud, discordant rendition of *Teddy Bears' Picnic.*

"This is a pathetic war machine," Nigel growled. "It seems its only weapon is this cataclysmic clattering. I'm not even certain of its effectiveness!"

"*War machine?*" Kayleesh mouthed to Nathan. Nathan shrugged, stifling a snigger.

"What are you two whispering about?" One of the weapon-wielding creatures demanded. His tone was surprisingly light and feminine.

"She said, *ice cream,*" lied Nathan. "We've not eaten since breakfast and this van is full of desserts."

"And how do you know that?"

"It's standard for a war machine to be well stocked with food full of energy," he said quickly.

"Well of course," the creature coughed. Ensuring that there was still a weapon pointing in Nathan and Kayleesh's direction, he stood up and soon spotted the chest freezer. He reached inside, delicately.

"Sir Nigel, would one like a Mivvi?"

CHAPTER 10

Nathan and Kayleesh clung to anything they could, to prevent themselves from being injured as the van swerved dangerously around bend after bend. It appeared that aliens, or Radiakkans at least, *were* able to drive ice cream vans. They just weren't very good at it. They had not been offered so much as a mini milk, but their interest soon waned when it was apparent that their captors were *wearing* more ice cream than they were managing to eat. Nathan was also feeling distinctly more travel sick than he had during any of his space flights. He swallowed.

Perhaps this *is how they're making everyone on Earth sick, with their horrendous driving.*

Above the din of the vehicle's inharmonious chimes, they could hear the occasional car horn blaring in protest at the hazardous van driver. Nathan was also convinced that he heard a police siren at one stage, although the driver seemed to escape it. How a police car could possibly manage to lose a pink and blue van blasting out nursery rhymes at a hundred decibels, he wasn't sure.

"Aagh!" The effeminate guard suddenly screamed. He dropped his weapon and put his hand to his head. "What is happening? The pain of it!"

"It looks like you've got brain freeze," Nathan observed.

"Brain freeze?" the Radiakkan's eyes grew wide. "Explain! And make it stop!"

"Aagh!" called out the other guard. "My brain is freezing too!"

"It's simple," said Nathan. "Just stop eating the ice cream. It'll soon pass."

As predicted, simultaneous expressions of relief spread over both their faces.

"What manner of foodstuff would *harm* the consumer?" the first guard said, crossly. "I am beginning to miss warm Radiakkan soup!"

Nathan and Kayleesh only laughed. Kayleesh seized her chance and reached for the fallen weapon. But it was quickly snatched from her grasp.

"Not so fast, elf-features!" He pushed the weapon against her head once more and restrained her. Kayleesh did not waste energy struggling.

The van came to a halt and the chiming ceased, mid-verse.

"Where are you taking us?" Kayleesh grumbled as they were removed from the van.

"We're taking you both out of harm's way."

"That's a shame. I wanted to meet the Supreme Ruler," said Kayleesh.

"The Supreme Ruler will not be arriving until…" began one of the men.

"Ssh!" hushed Nigel. "Don't tell them *anything*." He turned to Kayleesh. "The Supreme Ruler with not be available. And certainly not for the likes of *you*."

"Then we'll have to go through his deputy." Kayleesh winced as the guard who was escorting her, almost pulled her arm from its socket as he twisted it further round her back.

"You have no right to communicate with the Supreme Ruler, either through myself or otherwise."

"But we still have some questions to ask."

Nathan thought that Kayleesh was being very brave. She really didn't ever give up.

"You have asked enough questions!" Nigel barked. He was clearly getting extremely irritated.

"But we haven't received any answers!"

"Lock them in the east wing!" Nigel growled at the guards and stormed off alone, in the direction of what appeared to be a large manor house. The van driver followed him, striding purposefully up the gravel driveway.

"I know this place," Nathan whispered. "I used to come here when I was little. They had guided tours around the manor house and a maze in the grounds. I used to spend hours in that maze. It was owned by the Marquess and Marchioness of Hertford."

"I don't think they own it anymore," said Kayleesh, sadly.

"I wonder why they chose here and not the Houses of Parliament," he whispered.

"Where?"

"The Houses of Parliament - England's equivalent of the Wheylandian Parliamentary Building."

"I see. Well maybe they don't know about that – *I* didn't."

"Stop whispering, or we will carry out the threat we made earlier!"

The guards were walking rather awkwardly on the uneven ground and very close together, almost on top of each other. They actually clashed feet on several occasions. Nathan was not making the journey up the long gravel driveway an easy one for his captor. He was being dragged almost sideways, kicking up stones as he went.

He suddenly threw out a foot, caught the guard off-guard and managed to trip him up. Gravel scattered as he landed hard. The other guard toppled over him before he managed to stop himself. His momentum brought him crashing down onto the first guard with an almighty *oof.* It was a risk, he knew, but no bigger risk than rotting away in the east wing while they let the Earth be invaded. Kayleesh tumbled backwards onto the harsh ground, but Nathan's priority was to reach for the knife. Kayleesh, despite her fall, allowed herself an adrenalin-fuelled leap as she made for the weapons which had been thrown across the driveway on impact. With impeccable timing which surprised both of them, Kayleesh scooped up the weapons, threw one to Nathan. The pair of them brandished the knives. Nathan held a glistening blade at the guards who were struggling to their feet.

"Stay down for ten kroms… or you'll feel how sharp this blade is!"

The effeminate guard squealed, pathetically. The other guard grumbled at him to get up.

"I'm not getting my beautiful face slashed off!" he yelped.

"I'll slash your face off myself if you let those prisoners escape!" the other one threatened, gruffly.

"I'll inform Nigel! *Nigel! Nigel!*" he called out. His cries became muffled as his head was pushed into the pebbly ground by the other guard. Much kicking and yelling ensued as Nathan and Kayleesh took the opportunity to sneak away from the skirmish. Once on the soft, quiet grass, they sprinted across the grounds. They hadn't got very far, however, when Nathan heard the sound of footsteps running across the driveway.

"Follow me," Nathan panted. Their next obstacle, a cattle grid, lay between them and the adventure playground. They navigated across it and then headed in the direction of a dual zip wire. "Fancy a race?" Nathan grinned, grabbing hold of one of the ropes. Kayleesh grabbed the other rope and soon the two of them were speeding along the zip wires, away from the advancing guards. Kayleesh could not help but whoop with delight at the thrill of the ride. They came to a stop at the entrance to the maze and Nathan ushered her inside. The guards were mere distant specks.

"I can walk round this maze with my eyes closed and still find my way out. I know it as well as I know my own house."

"I'm very grateful for your local knowledge," Kayleesh panted. "First the Science and Discovery centre and now this strange place. What is it anyway?"

"Just a traditional folly really." Nathan shrugged. "The aim is to navigate through the labyrinth, find the centre, and then try and find your way out again."

"How odd. I just hope that those idiots can't find their way around it. There *is* just one other thing, Nathan."

"Yes?" Nathan turned another corner, never once meeting with a dead-end.

"You'll feel how sharp this blade is?" she mocked, and her shoulders shook with laughter.

"It's not something I ever thought I'd say, I must admit," laughed Nathan. "But I think we need to step up our game. I'm er... I'm assuming that neither of us has ever killed a man."

"Not me."

"Me neither. And we may not have to, but we might have to profess that we have the courage to from time to time. Even if we don't."

"Look, what exactly do you plan to do, take us to the centre of the maze and back out again?"

"I just want to lose them for now," Nathan said. They came to the end of a long straight and it seemed to Kayleesh that they were doubling back on themselves as they turned several corners in succession.

"And then we'll plan what to do next. One thing we *do* know is that this proposed *Supreme Ruler* is going to be in that very building at some point. If the Radiakkans in the vicinity are at the core of the invasion, then we're close to all the action. We have a chance."

"A chance of dying?"

"Well yes, maybe, but a chance to save the world. Ah, we're nearly there. Do you see the top of that tree?" Nathan pointed high above the wall. "That's where we're aiming for."

"Then why are we now heading in the opposite direction?"

"Don't worry. I know where we're going."

Tom Bowler opened the paska stone pot and admired its contents as they left Pappsie My's extraordinary emporium. An amber crystal, nestled inside a disc of precious-looking metal, glistened in the daylight. The shiny metal reminded him of his girlfriend's soft, golden hair. He vowed that he would see her again and that he would save them all. He closed the lid and placed the pot carefully in his pocket, next to the wrinkle-cream. They were wandering rather aimlessly around the village. Raphyl's craving for Truxxian gloop seemed to have passed and he was talking animatedly to Marry. Marry really seemed to have brought Raphyl out of himself; his energy seemed almost boundless. Gracer was walking along, peering in windows. Not just shop windows, but people's homes. She had even spotted someone in the bathtub, much to her amusement.

Tom's timepiece started to bleep.

"Tom, you need to get back to the ship." It was Ghy Hasprin. "We need to go back to Truxxe."

CHAPTER 11

"What?" Tom yelled at the timepiece. This was not the news he was waiting for. "We're going to Earth – you promised! As soon as the ship is fixed, we're going to *Earth!*"

"That was the plan," uttered a rather remorseful Ghy Hasprin.

"Then... then why are we not going there straight away? *Again?* Ghy? *Ghy?*" His timepiece was silent. It then started to bleep as Tom's heart rate accelerated. Tom tore it off in fury and dropped it into his pocket where the sound became muffled and then eventually ceased. "Gracer! Raphyl! We need to go back to the ship!"

"Already? I was going to look for somewhere where we could eat," said Gracer.

"I don't think we have time – Ghy has just called and summoned us all back. It sounds as though there's trouble on Truxxe."

"Truxxe? But we're going to Earth, aren't we?"

"We're *supposed* to be going to Earth. But Ghy said we have to go back to Truxxe. And then I lost him. Or he hung up on me. I suppose I was a bit rude to him, but he makes me so *angry* sometimes! This whole damn situation."

"I can imagine. I don't feel like going to Truxxe either," Gracer shuddered. "All I can think about is that creepy holoceiver incident!"

"You weren't technically on Truxxe then though," Raphyl pointed out. "Besides, they fired him anyway."

"That may be the case, but it was still a horrible thing to experience. And I'd rather go and save the Earth."

"Join the club!" said Tom.

"Why do we have to go to Truxxe?" asked one of the hatchlings.

"Let's go and find out," said Tom and broke into a sprint. The others followed suit.

They passed through the dusty, winding streets of the strange village.

"Bye Pappsie My," Gracer called out as they veered past his shop.

"Bye, strange wrinkle-cream lady," shouted Raphyl.

"Bye-bye, Ronnus," said Tom.

They ran over the soft, multi-coloured ground and down the hills, ALSID bot bobbing along behind them. One of the planet's three moons was sinking below the horizon. Distorted and broad, its mirror image amplified its majestic, blanched face as it dipped into the deep waters. The air was notably cooler now, and a bitter wind blew in the opposing direction, which made for an arduous journey. The youthful Marry over-took the puffing Tom Bowler as they neared the spacecraft.

There was no one to be seen.

Tom speculated that Ghy was inside. His prediction was correct.

"That was quick!" said Ghy.

"Well. you made it sound urgent," said Tom, slowly regaining his breath. Ghy simply smiled and gestured the party over to the mess hall. "So why do we have to go back now?"

"The Greys have found something at TSS. Something that they believe belongs to you."

"Me? Well, what could it be? I haven't been copying music illegally again. I have barely even been there!"

"It's a possession you brought with you."

"What?" Tom mentally unpacked the rucksack he had brought with him on his initial journey to Truxxe. "I don't understand. I haven't brought that much with me. Clothes, toiletries, reading material, a hand-held computer game; nothing offensive. What is it the Greys have found? Have I been framed or something? Because -"

"There's nothing to get defensive about, Tom. We'll go back to Truxxe, speak to the Greys and continue on to Earth."

"But we've just *come* from there! We've just gone in a huge circle for *nothing!*"

"Don't get angry, Tom. It's not Ghy's fault," Mayty Reeston rested a hand on his shoulder. But Tom had had enough. He shrugged off Mayty's hand. He didn't feel like being around any of them at the moment. He wanted to see Kayleesh and he wanted to go home. Why didn't anyone understand that? And why did the Greys want to bother him *again?* Tom didn't give them the pleasure of seeing him cry. Instead, he stomped off down the corridor. He stormed on passed the male quarters, searching for somewhere he could be alone. He eventually came across a row of storage lockers. Finding one just the right size he promptly swung it open, shut himself inside and sobbed.

It was growing dusky as Nathan and Kayleesh sat amongst the leafy branches of the tall horse chestnut tree. Kayleesh peeped through the twigs and looked across the maze. She started to giggle.

"What's so funny?" Nathan whispered, pushing a galling spiky conker shell away from his cheek.

"Those guards have come into the maze. I was worried that they might be able to see over the walls, but they're not quite tall enough. All I can see are the tops of two heads, occasionally bobbing up and down at different points.

"I don't think they can find *each other,* let alone the centre of the maze."

"They probably don't even know that they're supposed to be heading for the centre. They're most likely just wandering around, aimlessly."

"Even so, they're bound to reach this area eventually. Oh, Kayleesh, why did I even bring us up here? Now we're trapped! What a pillock."

"Don't panic, Nathan. Maybe we can trap them somehow, knock them out or something."

"Yes, we could ambush them! Quick, gather some of these conkers."

"What, these spiky things?" Kayleesh touched one of them, heedfully.

"Yes. Be careful. Maybe we could store them in your hat." They had soon gathered enough conkers to fill Kayleesh's hat. Nathan pulled on the nearest branch. It rustled, noisily, as it swayed. He cried out in a mocking tone, "I bet you can't find us..." The two of them giggled and then stayed absolutely still, as they observed two heads, bobbing at a faster rate.

The gruff one called out in annoyance. Nathan couldn't understand what he was saying, however. Perhaps the adventure playground was outside of the influence of the nearest ALSID. The guard ducked into the courtyard and looked about him, hands on hips. He muttered something to himself, rather crossly. The guard seemed to notice the tree for the first time and, as he looked up, a hard, spiked object hit him right in the eye. Before he had time to react, another hit him squarely on the chin. There was an incoherent bout of protestations and much arm waving, when a particularly large third projectile caught the softest part of his cranium and he fell to the ground.

The other guard poked his head through the only exit. Startled at the site of his fallen comrade, he knelt beside him. He squealed his way through several words. Suddenly, something fell on the ground beside him. He picked it up and then looked up into the tree, eyes narrow and lips pursed. He shouted something and then hurled the conker in the direction of the horse chestnut tree's uppermost branches. There came a small yelp. Turning back to the motionless guard, he spied another conker, picked it up and aimed it at the tree. Before he had chance to cast his weapon, however, two more came hurtling down towards him.

His limp body slumped over, squashing the other guard beneath him.

"They're very close, those too," Nathan tittered from the treetop. "Come on. Let's tie them to the tree before they wake up."

"What with?"

"There are some rope swings in the playground, and I have my knife," said Nathan. "Stay here and make sure they don't wake up."

"How am I going to do that?"

"Your hat is empty, but it looks as though the tree will allow for another round or two. Collect some more ammunition!" He was already clambering down the tree trunk, tossing up the occasional conker he happened to come across on his descent.

Nathan skirted past the snoozing Radiakkans and retraced his steps through the maze. Even in the dark, he soon found the exit. He ran across the playground and unsheathed the knife as he neared the rope swings.

But metal had hard barely touched rope when a cold hand clasped around his mouth. He struggled momentarily, but this time his captor was no bumbling guard. Nathan's body relaxed. The cold hand around his mouth jerked away. The pherobot turned to face him.

Although he was not restrained and the pherobot gave him no instruction, Nathan felt compelled to follow him. They walked silently across the adventure playground, through the grounds and further and further away from the maze; further away from Kayleesh. Once they reached close proximity of the house, the pherobot finally spoke. His metallic voice rang genially in Nathan's ears. He felt almost comforted by the frosty, crudely built android.

"You will follow me to the east wing where you will remain until you are summoned."

"Certainly," said Nathan. He found the pherobot's tones so welcoming and his presence so amiable and comforting that he found it impossible to disagree. He followed obediently as he was led in through a side entrance to the grand mansion. The pherobot's steps clanged on stone as they ascended a narrow spiral staircase which had historically been reserved for the use of serving staff. At the end of a long hallway, an oak door was unlocked, and

Nathan was pushed into a sparsely furnished bedroom. The door slammed shut behind him. He stared at the other side of the oak door and blinked. He remained there for several minutes until the behavioural field had moved on.

Suddenly he looked about him, filled with a flurry of panicked thoughts:

What is happening? Why did I follow that thing? I don't even remember how I got here so how am I going to find my way out? - and then - *Kayleesh!*

He pulled ineffectively at the doorknob, began pacing the room and then attempted to tackle the doorknob again. He peered out of the room's only window. He was three floors up. He cursed and began pacing again.

Hannond Putt was feeling rather dismayed that his efforts to prise open one of the barrels had been wasted.

"Bah!" he shouted. "They're not filled with whiskey after all. It's merely some odourless clear stuff."

"As I suspected," said Schlomm. "However, we can't drink the shipment."

"It would only have been one barrel."

"As much as I am beginning to like this more rebellious Hannond since his return from Porriduum, the order is from *Radiakka.* If it was from any other race I would have dumped the entire payload in one of Andromeda's outer spiral arms days ago. But if we lose just one drop of this liquid, I'm confident that there would be consequences."

"How much further?"

"Another few hours yet. I have a small bottle of Glorbian Whiskey in my quarters if you want to fetch that. It should make the rest of the journey pass a little more swiftly."

Hannond grinned and padded off down the corridor.

Tom Bowler crept into the male sleeping quarters. The room resounded with stores and grunts, but he couldn't have remained in the storage locker any longer. It had been cramped and uncomfortable and he had no more tears left to soak the bed pillow. He curled up on his bunk, foetal-like and drifted into dreamless sleep.

CHAPTER 12

Tom Bowler spent most of the journey back to Truxxe lying on his bunk, facing the wall. He wasn't in the mood for conversation and socialising. He was too sad, anxious and frustrated. Sad because he missed Kayleesh, anxious about what was going to happen when he met with the Greys at TSS and frustrated that he still couldn't get to Earth. He was conscious of the fact that Raphyl and Ghy had come into the room, on occasion, and had tried to talk to him. But each time he had feigned sleep. He also knew that the Menilles had also braved the male quarters once or twice, as he had heard them chatter and try to wake him. But he remained there, only getting out of bed to find something to eat when the others slept, until the ship finally docked at the planetoid's service station. And then he moved with great reluctance.

When he finally set foot on Truxxe ground, he was not met with the troop of angry Greys he was expecting. Instead, he was greeted by Hyganty and Frarrk. Hyganty waved a pincer, beckoning him over through the crowded space port. Confused, Tom went over to the green, praying mantis creatures and greeted them both.

"Thank you for coming back so quickly," Hyganty clicked.

"What do you mean? We were summoned back by the Greys. We were on our way to Earth when Ghy got the message."

"Ghy got the message from me," said Hyganty.

"From *you?* But..."

"Let me explain. The Greys *did* find something of yours. Something you brought onto the TSS Transit Ship on your first journey here. They don't know what it is. Once they realised that it was nothing dangerous, Frarrk managed to persuade them to release it."

"What is it?"

"Come with us to floor seventy-six and you can tell us," said Frarrk. "It is no longer impounded. It's being kept in a holding area."

"We'll come with you," Gracer said. Tom hadn't even realised that she and Raphyl were standing behind him. "Don't worry it won't be too crowded; Marry wants to visit the Express Cuisine."

Tom had never visited floor seventy-six before. In fact, there were many levels of the station which Tom had not visited. He surmised that Raphyl hadn't been there before either as he seemed to be looking about him and taking in the dark walls lined with flashing holographic images of various items; hats, timepieces and melody mechs. It was as though they were inside a colossal lost property bin. Gracer tried one of the doors which ran along the long corridor. There was a holographic image of a rather lavish pair of shoes flashing on the wall next to it.

"We only have access to one of these rooms," Hyganty informed her.

"Worth a try," Gracer sighed.

An image of a bicycle caught Tom's eye. Frarkk used a card to access the room adjacent to it. They stepped inside.

It was Tom's bicycle.

"I thought... I thought I'd left this back on Earth. I left it in the field when I got on the ship," said Tom. He inspected the bicycle, trying to determine whether anything had been tampered with. "The ship must have picked it up that day. But why? And why didn't they tell me?"

"Perhaps they didn't know what it was," suggested Gracer. Hyganty looked at him, cocked his head to one side, obviously ridden with curiosity.

"What is it, Tom?" he said, in a voice caked in seriousness.

"What *is it?*" Tom choked. He absent-mindedly tried the brakes and hopped onto the saddle. "It's my bike."

"What is it for? Is it for cutting crops? Some kind of transmitter? A weapon?"

"A weapon? No, no, no. It's a vehicle!"

"A vehicle?"

"Yeah. I haven't got my diving licence yet, so I used to get around on this." By way of demonstration he pedalled a few wobbly feet across the holding room then squeezed the brakes.

"How extraordinary!" exclaimed Frarrk. "I'm interested in other-worldly artefacts."

"Is that why you brought me all the way back here? For a *bicycle?*"

"We thought it might be important to you," said Hyganty. "And we weren't sure that it wasn't dangerous until a couple of hours ago. We had to convene with the Greys, who are not the easiest people to deal with, and we thought it best that you come back and regain it as quickly as possible."

"I was about to save the Earth and you bring me back here for a two-hundred quid racing bike?"

"What did you say?"

"Tom's planet is in danger," Raphyl explained. "We were on a mission to save it."

"I thought you were on a spotoon tour," Frarkk's feelers waved in the air.

"We were. Well, we were travelling in the ship Hasprin's Legion had use of to get to Earth."

"While having a few games of spotoon along the way?"

"Well... yes. It was the only way."

"That seems like an odd way of saving the world," said Frarrk.

"It's not how we'd go about it," Hyganty scoffed.

"Well you weren't around to help when we needed you and, excuse me, but I'm not in the habit of saving the world. It's not something I am required to do on a daily basis. I don't have a protocol in place," said Tom, his anger getting the better of him again.

"I'm sorry Tom. We're here now. And we will help you."

"You will?"

"Of course... if we can."

"It looks like we've got quite an army on our side now!" Grinned Gracer.

"What do you want us to do?" asked Frarrk.

"Your ship – we can use that to get to Earth!"

Frarrk looked at Hyganty.

"We... we no longer have the Submian ship."

"What?" said Raphyl. "I loved that ship!" His shoulders fell.

"Well, it wasn't strictly our ship."

"We *borrowed* it for one of our missions and we failed to give it back."

"You stole that spaceship?" Raphyl whooped. "I'm impressed! Wow guys, I always thought you two were quite square-toed. I didn't think stealing a spacecraft was your thing."

"We're not as we seem," Hyganty said. "That is how we conduct our missions. We are part of the conspiracy theorists guild after all."

"That makes sense," said Gracer.

"It does?" asked a perplexed Tom. "Anyway, what happened? Didn't you get arrested for the theft?"

"We have a suspended sentence – one more pincer out of place and it's Porriduum for us."

"So, Tom went to the worst prison planet for thousands of light-years for illegally copying one of my melody cards and you two steal a hulking great military ship and get to walk away?"

"Submians are more lenient than Radiakkans," Frarrk stated.

"I'll say!"

"But this still means that we have to be extra careful with how we go about things. We can't risk Hyganty and Frarkk being sent to that place," said Tom.

"Where is the beautiful Kayleesh?" asked Hyganty. Tom flinched. He had not forgotten how he had been jealous of the Submian's friendship with Kayleesh, when they were discussing the origins of Truxxe. He also remembered how much he was missing her.

"Kayleesh and Nathan are on Earth. Let's go to Bar Six Seven and we'll tell you all about it."

Raphyl gave a cheer.

"Very well. The Greys will authorise the release of your property now that you can verify it. Why don't you take your vehicle back to your apartment on the way?"

A rather tipsy Hannon Putt waddled his way off the Cluock II. He was humming a terrible Glorbian tune which had managed to chart at the number one spot for seventy-five consecutive weeks.

"What have I told you about singing that song?" a grumpy Schlomm growled out of the mouth of the spaceship. He rolled a keg down the ramp, narrowly missing his brother.

"I wasn't singing it. I was humming it!"

"I'll be humming the Glorbian funeral march if you don't shut up. Now help me with these barrels."

"Aren't we going to introduce ourselves first?"

"Let's just get the consignment delivered as soon as possible and get our money, shall we? The Radiakkans aren't interested in niceties. And neither am I."

"Where are we anyway? It looks as though we're in some sort of courtyard."

"That's because it *is* a courtyard. It's some kind of human abode for the wealthy."

"It's pretty impressive." Hannond padded around the ship, taking in the high stone walls and gardens richly adorned with polished sculptures and vibrant flora. "I wonder if it was designed by Authority Construction Designs."

"It's unlikely. The Radiakkans inform me that this human planet is ignorant to other worlds. Why am I discussing such trivia with you anyway? Let's get this shipment delivered."

Nathan Reed woke up. He threw back the threadbare blanket which offered the only protection against the chill of the unheated room. His gaze fell on the crooked table which had served as his meal place since his imprisonment. He had been too late. *Again.* A tray containing barely enough food to sustain him throughout the day had been left there while he had slept. He had planned to stay awake and ambush his soft-footed waiter, but he had been too weak and tired, and sleep had again taken him. He didn't know why he felt as weak as he did. He wasn't eating as much as his growling stomach demanded, but his energy expenditure since he had been kept captive, had been minimal.

Pulling the itchy blanket tightly around him, Nathan fetched the breakfast tray, which also contained his lunch and dinner. He sat down on the lumpy bed. The tray bore the same offerings as it had the previous day. And the day before that. He glugged half of a pitcher of water, crammed a bread roll into his mouth and tore at the measly helping of sliced ham. He saved the rotting pear and meagre portion of rancid cheese for later in the day. In case he got desperate. And he knew that he would. He wasn't sure how long he'd been locked up in the old servants' quarters. Days? Weeks? All he knew was that his whiskers had turned beard and his slop bucket was three-quarters full.

As he placed the unsavoury items back on the crooked table, he heard a voice which grabbed his attention.

Kayleesh? No, I am not myself. I am so weak and confused that I am starting to hear things. But it sounded so much like her...

He was about to call out, but his body had other ideas. He reached for the bucket and his stomach lurched. Up came the bread roll and up came the ham.

On no, not me too! I can't get ill as well! Was it because I was in contact with my mum? And then Dad?

Nathan lay back on the bed, his stomach empty and his head throbbing.

CHAPTER 13

"Got you!" Nathan cried out. It had taken all of his energy and all of his will to stay awake. He now had his early-rising waiter trapped under the old blanket. He used all of his might to keep whoever it was, pinned to the oak floor. They were wriggling and screaming. It sounded like a female. The breakfast tray she had been carrying was poking out of the blanket. Intrigued, Nathan picked it up and held it aloft, before tearing back the cover.

A cowering Kayleesh lay shaking on the floor. The tray clanged to the floor.

"You're the one who's been bringing me food?"

"I had to... they made me work for them. But they wouldn't let me wake you."

"All this time?" Nathan slumped to the floor. Kayleesh nodded.

"They're keeping me here too, in a closet room by the kitchens. They found me in the maze and now they've been forcing me to work and prepare them food." Kayleesh wiped a teary eye. "Nathan, I will have to go. If they think I've been talking to any of the prisoners, they will really hurt me."

It was then that Nathan noticed a large, purple bruise on her arm. There was another on her leg which had faded to yellow. How long had they been there? Nathan nodded, open-mouthed.

"How many prisoners are there?"

"A few.... well there were... most of them got sick... look, I really have to go!" Kayleesh got to her feet. Nathan grabbed her arm. She winced.

"Kayleesh, there's something you need to know. I'm sick too. Like my Mum and Dad. Like all of them."

"Not you too!"

Nathan nodded. He let her go. Even after she had closed the door, he could hear her sobs echoing all the way down the corridor. He threw the blanket onto the bed and gathered up the tray and provisions. The water pitcher had completely emptied, and the bread was sodden. Too angry and nauseous to eat anything, he sat back on the bed. Head in his hands, he stared at the floor. What was he going to do?

And what was that digging into him?

Nathan felt underneath his leg and found something cold and metallic.

A key!

Nathan didn't know whether Kayleesh had purposefully left it for him or if it had fallen into the blanket when he had ambushed her, but he smiled for the first time in days. Finding renewed strength, Nathan crept to the door and tried the doorknob. It was locked. So Kayleesh *had* left a spare one. *Well done Kayleesh!* He fumbled at the keyhole and he felt the key turn. He let the door creak open, just enough for him to discover that the key worked. One small glimpse of the world outside the room made Nathan want nothing more than to escape, but his mind was not functioning properly, and he didn't have the strength to run today. Of course, the sickness might weaken him further still with time, but it was a risk that he would need to take. He forced himself to eat the rancid cheese and fruit and slept for twelve long hours.

Raphyl, Gracer Menille, Tom Bowler, Hyganty and Frarrk were occupying a corner booth in Bar Six Seven. The Truxxian was glugging down a large tripedal glass full of Truxxian gloop, his tongue darting around the perimeter of the glass as though he was afraid to lose one drop. Gracer was enjoying a tray heaped with bar snacks which she was shovelling into her mouth with glee. Tom wondered whether her huge appetite was indicative of her spawning her next clutch of eggs, or whether she was just simply pleased to eat something other than the over-processed space flight food to which they'd recently become accustomed. Hyganty and Frarrk sipped cocktails, in a strange, kindred fashion. They even placed their glasses down at the same time between sips. Tom was drinking his usual beverage and picking at a bowl of what he had thought was olives, but their appearance had been deceptive. He pulled a face at the tart, grape-like flavour and pushed the bowl in Gracer's direction. They were readily vacuumed up along with the rest of her bounty, as Tom told the Submians of how they had lost Nathan and Kayleesh and of their adventures on Jaloosh and Ronnus.

"Ah, Ronnus," said Hyganty. "I have heard of that strange place. Maybe I should visit it one day."

"You really should," slurred Raphyl. "For you really have to see it to believe it. As for that wrinkle-cream that lady was selling – completely crazy!"

"Wrinkle cream?" asked Frarrk. Tom produced the pot and placed it on the table.

"Whatever do they put in this?" Frarkk examined the pot between his pincers.

"And why?" questioned Gracer.

"You're welcome to analyse it, Frarrk" shrugged Tom. "I don't think it's much of a gift for my girlfriend."

"If you're sure. It is an intriguing product."

"Oh yes, I have something much more special for Kayleesh."

Tom reached into his pocket for the paska stone pot. But the reveal was interrupted by a rather distraught-looking pair of Truxxians. Chazner and Ransel appeared at the booth. The pot-bellied spotoon players were panting, their purple neck veins pulsating. Furthermore, they didn't offer Tom the Hasprin's Legion salute, so Tom knew that something was wrong.

"Hey, Hasprin's Legionites," Raphyl cheered, oblivious. "We need to use the spotoon-mobile again. We need to get to Earth, there is no other way, especially as we no longer have use of the amazing Submian ship."

"I don't think that's going to be possible," Ransel gulped. "We've just come back from the Clinicarium on floor seventeen."

"The helmsmen of the *spotoon-mobile,* as you call it, are very sick. As are the rest of the spotoon team," said Chazner.

"Ghy and Mayty are ill?" cried Tom. "What's wrong with them all?"

"They all appear to have the same sickness. They've been vomiting since we landed."

"I think Ghy felt ill when we were on the ship," said Ransel. "I don't think he wanted to admit it, being the strong leader that he is, but not long after we left Ronnus he wasn't himself and he didn't always join us at meal-times."

"And it's most unlike Ghy to miss a meal," Chazner added.

"I didn't notice... I was too busy sulking," sighed Tom. "I was so selfish and stupid..."

"Let's go to the Clinicarium," Gracer said.

"No!" protested Raphyl. "I don't want to get sick too!"

"If it was contagious then we would have been ill by now, wouldn't we?"

"I'm not sure. There's not really any evidence to suggest either," said Tom.

"I don't think we should risk it," said Raphyl, who was onto his second drink.

"How are you two feeling after your visit?" Hyganty wondered.

"I feel all right," shrugged Chazner.

"Me too," said Ransel. "And Medic Flonce didn't say that we should stay away."

"That's a good point," said Chazner. "Well I don't know about you lot, but at times like this I like to lose myself in a game of spotoon. Will anyone join me?" Only Ransel responded with an affirmative. It was evident that more important issues were afoot for Tom and his friends. "Very well. See you later." The two of them left the booth and approached the game disc.

"Poor Ghy and the others," sighed Gracer. She pushed away her empty tray and wiped her mouth. "I wonder what happened. Did they pick something up while working on the ship?"

"Mayty didn't work on the ship – he went to relax in the brine lakes," remembered Tom.

"Very strange. I hope they soon recover."

"So, do you think they'll let us use the ship?" asked Raphyl.

"Unlikely. The team was lucky enough to have use of it in the first place," said Tom. "Plus, the helmsmen are all ill."

"So, what is our next move?" asked Hyganty.

"I don't know. I really don't know," sighed Tom. "But it's times like this that I like to go for a ride and think."

"You like to what?" asked Raphyl.

"I'm going to go back to my quarters and get my bicycle."

Nathan Reed ducked behind an antique cabinet, ensuring that the hallway remained empty before he proceeded. He had carefully closed the bedroom door, taking care to make it look as though the bed was occupied, by placing an assortment of items from the room underneath the blanket. The final effect was rather lumpy and misshapen, but it was the best he could do under the circumstances. The twilit house was quiet and still. He crawled over to the room next door to the one he had been locked in and tried the key. Fortuitously, the key turned in the lock and the door crept slowly open. He clamped a hand to his mouth as the stench hit him like a putrid wall. On the bed lay a well-dressed gentleman, his attire lustrous and affluent. Next to him lay a slender noblewoman, dressed in opulent apparel, her neck dripping with diamonds. The scene was not one of repose and luxury, however, for the twain were lying on a vomit-sodden bed sheet. The motionless couple were close, their hands interlocked.

Is this the Marquess and Marchioness?

Nathan backed out of the room, for the image was too distressing to behold any longer. Nathan closed the door behind him and breathed. Despite feeling unsettled,

Nathan didn't want to leave until he had tried the other doors. He hoped to find someone alive, someone he could rescue. The skeleton key opened four more rooms, all empty, all bearing the same stench of vomit, faeces and death. The bodies had evidently been removed. Between each room Nathan crouched, waited, bided his time, ensured he had not been spotted. But why had the bodies of the Marquess and Marchioness been left for so long? Surely they would have been the first ones to have been held prisoner. In their own home. Perhaps the Radiakkans wanted to keep the bodies for something. He remembered how the Wheylandians had treated Raghael and Mirrie, their frozen bodies preserved as trophies in the grounds of the Parliamentary Building for centuries. Nathan shuddered. Perhaps they would find something equally horrifying to do with these two, particularly if they believed humans held them in high esteem.

Nathan crumpled to the ground when he faced what was in the final room. For lying in the middle of the floor, was the body of an infant. The child who could not have been old enough to attend school, was as richly clad as the Marquess and Marchioness, and just as inanimate. The boy's small hands were clasped around a piece of rotting fruit, his mop of red hair was lank, and his clothes were soiled. Nathan found it a challenge to stifle his own bawling. Then sadness gave way to anger. Determination goaded him on, and a renewed strength rose within him. He would help to avenge these terrible deaths.

How many people have you done this to? How many children? We'll stop you, before you can do any more damage!

Alone, Nathan retreated from the room and stood flat against the wall.

Still silent.

He felt the gentle pull of a pherobot's influence.

Not now, not now!

The sensation faded. He assumed that a patrolling android had passed along the corridor on a floor below. He realised that he could use this sense to detect where the android was. As long as he could resist its influence and he didn't get too close to the field then he would be safe. At the top of the stairs, he waited. Two minutes later he felt the pull again. He felt obligated to follow and to surrender, but he resisted, his fingernails digging deep into the bannister in physical self-restraint. Another two minutes passed and the same feeling again. He could not hear the *clunk clunk* of the pherobot's feet on stone, so Nathan gauged that there was at least a floor between them. Gingerly, he descended to the floor below and explored the corridor. A sudden clanging of metal panicked him. But it sounded like metal on metal. The smell of baking bread confirmed his hunch. But none of the doors would open, by handle nor key.

I expect the kitchen would be on the ground floor, pondered Nathan. *But I can't get to it without getting too close to the pherobot field. Or can I?*

Two minutes more passed, but Nathan did not feel the influence of the behavioural field. He waited a minute longer.

Maybe it's gone down to the cellar.

He took the risk and tiptoed down the next level, one worn stone step at a time.

"Nathan!" A familiar voice greeted him and Kayleesh ushered him into the kitchen. "You're OK!"
Kayleesh threw her arms around her friend. She looked as though she had been crying again. "You do look pale though. Here, have some of the soup I've been making for the Radiakkans." She offered him a bowl. "It's all they seem to eat. And its proper food – not like the scraps I was made to serve you. They didn't want me to give you meat by the way - I had to sneak that onto your tray."

Nathan smiled at her and took a seat in the shadows at the back of the room. He enjoyed spoonful after spoonful of warm, creamy broth before placing down the empty bowl.

"We need to get out of here. I can feel the pull of the pherobot."

"I'll lock you in the cupboard so that you can't act on your compulsions as it passes."

"Won't the pherofield affect you?"

"It'll only compel me to make more soup."

"I think I can live with that."

Tom Bowler tied a glow rock to the handlebars of his bicycle. The tyres were partially deflated, and the uncertain ground did not make for an easy ride, but he didn't mind. The physical exertion aided to free his mind for clear thinking. The peddling human, a moving pool of light, travelled away from the service station and out into the wilderness. The air was still, and the sky was darker than ever. As the distance between he and TSS became greater, the quieter and darker it became. His breath in the starry day was all that he could hear. He felt free and in control for the first time in a long while. He was finally in control of his own destiny, at least for the next few hours. He could ride through rocky ravines, travel out far onto the planes and explore vast lands for as long he wished; or at least until he got a puncture. The choice was his own. He rode faster, standing on the pedals and crouching forward as he used to, feeling the breeze on his cheeks. He thought about nothing but the bike and where he chose to steer it. At one point he could see the dome of the largest building which dominated the town of Canmar Three, a Truxxian university town Tom had visited before. He recalled the trip where he had visited the Job Selector in an attempt to get a job on Porriduum so that he could reach Raphyl. He laughed at the irony. The cluster of buildings looked so beautiful on the horizon – cosy and inviting. But Tom steered away and continued along his own track. He cycled for almost a mile over grassland and then back through a large cluster of glimmering glow rocks, changed direction again and steered around swampland. The terrain was becoming more and more varied and Tom eventually realised that he was approaching Crossvein Tourist Centre.

He was beginning to tire and decided that a break was in order.

Tom remembered that TSS staff passes granted free access to all of the centre's amenities. He parked his bike with the row of ALSID bots which were waiting outside for their owners' return and entered the tall building. He remembered the large lounge area and the smell of the plush furnishings. Staff members, robed in red, were handing out leaflets and drinks to customers. Tom didn't need the introductory tour. He just wanted to be somewhere other than TSS where he could be alone and think. He showed his pass to an attendant and entered the museum. There were a handful of people in the dome-topped room. He idly walked around the perimeter, his fingers lightly touching the railing as he went. The railing was all that lay between the visitors and the five metre drop in the centre of the circular room. He passed the exhibits which he had surveyed on his previous visit which buzzed into life at his presence, but he paid them little regard.

"Truxxe, the wandering planetoid, spinning in the cosmos, its unique perpetual rotation a mystery to scientists today..."

Tom had felt that his mind was clearer and here he had the space to think. He had no spaceship, no money for a Holoceiver and he was running out of time. He pondered.

There has to be another way.

He passed the exhibition which had upset him so much on his previous visit. He remembered how he had been faced with images of poverty and had left before seeing the remainder of the exhibition. How long ago that seemed. He considered how many things he had seen since that day. This time, however, he moved on to the next display which clicked into action.

A holographic video illuminated above a rather impressive looking stone podium. The hologram showed how Crossvein Tourist Centre was constructed. The video was accelerated, with different angles being shown simultaneously to a backdrop of extraordinary music. There were too many images to focus on any of them properly, but two particular images did catch Tom's attention. He was convinced that he saw a flash of the chamber in which he was standing. It was at the early building stages and there was no roof. In the other image, the camera panned down to the centre of the circular room, but instead of the smooth, concave base in the centre, there seemed to be a pit which went down and down. There was a glimmer of something down there, but Tom could not make out what it was. The image was too fast and of too poor quality. His eyes darted about the holographic whirr as he attempted to make out anything else of interest. But all too soon the finished edifice lay before him, spinning triumphantly to a fanfare, in stark contrast to the previous exhibit.

There was some commentary relating to employment and trade, but nothing was mentioned about the time when there was no roof and no proper foundation and when the building was merely a shell. Tom wasn't even sure why he was so intrigued by the images, but there was something about them that seemed wrong. What was down there? He stepped over to the railing and peered over the edge; and saw nothing but a smooth, concave pit. He knew of a few skateboarders who would have been thrilled at the sight. *Maybe I should have brought my bike in!*

The final exhibit burst back into life as two Truxxian children approached it. Tom watched again, his heart pumping faster and faster.

There is definitely something down there! But what?

CHAPTER 14

Tom bided his time until the end of the day and hung around, pretending to be casually viewing the exhibits, whenever a customer came into the chamber. As his timepiece struck the eighth hour, a Truxxian and two Lymice exited the chamber, leaving Tom finally alone in the room. The chamber lighting dimmed to half its intensity. Tom did not want to risk getting caught loitering by anyone closing up the museum for the night, so he ducked behind the stone podium and waited a while longer. He *had* to find out more about the museum, about the pit.

Sure enough, Tom heard the entrance open and close. Slow, deliberate footsteps circled around the entire hall, and Tom waited for them to pass. Finally, the exit door opened and banged shut. The sound resonated around the hollow space. As Tom crept away from his hiding place, the lighting faded to black and he was left alone in the vast darkness.

Tom noticed that his pocket was glowing, however, and he reached into it and produced the small glow rock he had stowed there. Tom grinned and kissed the nugget.

Always carry a spare! He held the glow rock in front of him and found his way over to the railing. He waved it about, in order to get a better view of the concave pit. But he could still see no way inside; it was seamless. He wanted to drop down and take a closer look, but he knew that he would never be able to find purchase on the smooth stone; he'd be trapped. He pondered.

I'm missing something. I found my way out of Porriduum, and that place was enormous. And deadly. If only Ragghael and Mirrie had designed this building, then I might have a better idea of how its cryptic system worked - if there even is a cryptic system. Maybe I should have brought them with me. Perhaps that's the answer. If I leave now – that's assuming I am not locked in – I can come back with them tomorrow.

But as Tom made his way towards the exit, the glow from the small stone picked something out in one of the recesses along the wall. It was the recess which was home to the unfavourable exhibit. Tom approached, but the exhibit didn't whir into life as it typically would. Tom realised that all of the exhibits must have been deactivated. The lack of activity was disconcerting. Tom held the rock out in front of him. His pulse throbbed through his system as he waved the rock around. Unrecognisable symbols shifted and glowed on the concave surface of the wall recess. He reached out, but his quaking fingers felt nothing but level stone. What were the symbols? And why wasn't the ALSID translating them? The symbols shifted again, finally into a familiar shape, *B*.

Excitedly, Tom ran to the next recess and waved the stone until the light picked up another shifting symbol. As the ALSID translated the text, the shape settled on *D*. Grinning inanely, but not thoroughly understanding, he approached the next recess; nothing. Far from being discouraged, however, he tackled all of the recesses in the chamber. Five of them revealed glowing inscriptions, *B, D, C, E, A, F, G.* His logical mind pleaded with him to alphabetise them. But how? He visited each of them in turn; pushing his hand against the inscriptions in turn; *A, B, C, D, E, F* then *G*. He wasn't sure what he was trying to achieve, but it had to be a message, didn't it? Frustrated, Tom leaned against recess *B* and threw the glow rock up in the air and caught it several times, as he reflected. Perhaps the letters spelled something.

Eight inscriptions… eight letters… or... eight notes? Maybe the letters don't have to be alphabetised – maybe they have to be played.

Tom punched the air. But then his fist morphed into a palm and he slapped his forehead for the realisation of lack of a musical instrument.

What am I supposed to do? Whip out a recorder and dance a jig as I play a couple of bars of music?

He gave out a long scream in desperation.

Ping!

"Ping?" he said, aloud. And then "Ouch!"

He reeled quickly around for his back was searing. The letter *B* was glowing and pulsating brighter than ever as he passed the glow rock over the surface of the recess. Heat was resonating from the inscription.

"What woke *you* up?" asked Tom, inquisitively. He pressed the letter, but this achieved nothing other than a hissing sound and slightly sautéed fingers. He shouted out in pain before blowing on his cooked flesh.

Pong!

"Pong? Now look here, stop messing with my head, room, and give me a less painful way of saying whatever it is you're trying to say!" At the edge of his vision, Tom noticed that the *A* in one of the recesses at the other side of the chamber was glowing brightly. "What?" He screamed out in desperation again; a scream which happened to reach exactly the same pitch as his original holler.

Ping!

"OK so we now have Ping and Pong. Are you going to torture me, room, with varying degrees of pain until I scream an entire concerto?"

Tom saw that the *A* was cooling and fading in the distance. He turned to see that *B,* also, was fading.

So now both A and B have been deactivated – I wonder if it was because I got the sequence wrong? I need to hit B through to G, with all of the correct notes in between. Whoever devised this game must surely have had a strange mind, but to what end? Is this some kind of combination lock, I wonder? And now that I've figured it out, how am I supposed to correctly reach all of the notes? A professional singer might be able to do it first time, but this is not really my forte.

Nevertheless, Tom attempted to sing the combination lock into action. His first attempt failed. He tried again, and five of the eight symbols glowed hot and orange, but he rushed the *G* note and sang a semitone higher than required. He cursed himself. *I'm not a singer!* He half expected a camera crew and a bearded presenter to appear from behind the large podium at any moment. *This is crazy!*

Tom took a deep breath, took his time and ran through the notes once again. With each correct note, one by one, the letters came to life until finally all eight of them stayed lit. He punched the air again in triumph.

Tom made a grab for the railing as the floor beneath him suddenly began to rumble and quake. But the railing didn't prove to assist him as it warped and bowed in his hands. In spite of this, he clung on, but he lost his footing and blundered over the edge and slid down the slippery walls of the pit. His knuckles white, Tom prised himself off the rail and tried to steady himself. As soon as he managed to stand upright, however, the floor beneath him crumbled away and he scrambled desperately for purchase.

Tom plunged into the darkness.

Nathan Reed and Kayleesh, their stomachs full of broth, were finally out of the influence of the pherofield. They had succeeded in escaping from the servants' quarters, but they had still not found their way out of the invaders' headquarters.

"I don't think we should escape. Not yet," whispered Kayleesh as the pair sidled down a narrow passageway.

"What? Do you want us to get killed?"

"I don't think we're any safer in the grounds than in here, do you?"

"Perhaps not, but what do you propose we do?"

"We need to find out what's going on. We need to find out the Radiakkans' next move. Maybe if we find out where all of the discussions are taking place and listen in, we can get some information."

"Are the Radiakkans really the type of people who would hold meetings and pass around the conference sweets? I thought they were more brutal."

"Oh no. They're a shrewd, guileful, deceitful race. And most of the ones in this building are politicians. Of course, they hold meetings! While I was serving them breakfast yesterday morning, they were discussing a meeting which is to be held today. I think that it might be a major one because one of them commented on the amount of soup that they need to feed extra attendees."

"Perhaps we could disguise ourselves so that we could get into one of their meetings unnoticed."

"You want me to disguise myself as a human, disguised as a Radiakkan?"

"I think your human disguise fell by the wayside some time ago," Nathan said and tapped her elfin ear which was protruding through her golden locks."

"But maybe we could still sneak in. I wonder if the meeting will be held in the dining room where I've been serving them. It *is* quite large."

"I'm thinking bigger," said Nathan. "Do you know where the ballroom is?"

Tom Bowler brushed dust and debris from his clothing and squinted in the blackness. He looked around for the glowrock, but a much brighter light irradiated the pit. He gasped and stared up at the huge hologram which glimmered before him. Luminescent and immense, the hologram depicted a seated Luenian; the illusion made it appear to be seated on a real rock below the projection. The dark red bipedal creature was imposing and magnificent. Its proud, muscular tail was coiled around its base and the end of the tail waved in a slow and controlled manner. The creature was dressed in cream, like the ones Tom had met on Leuania, but the costume had more of an official air about it, as though he was an officer or perhaps an academic.

Tom stepped backwards, struggling to get the entire image in his field of vision. He craned his neck and stared up at the towering figure. The quiescent image simply glared ahead, unseeing, unblinking. Tom waved and jumped around, endeavouring to catch its attention. He surmised that the figure could not see him.

"Hello?" Tom called out, his voice echoing. Still, the figure remained motionless and staid. He hoped that this Luenian's temperament was closer to that of Cass Harble, who he had befriended on the planet, than to the hostile guards he had encountered. "I'm not going to give up. I'm not going to give up on defeating the Radiakkans and I'm not going to give up on saving the Earth."

Nothing.

"And I went to a lot of trouble activating you. So can you please explain what this is all about?"

Silence.

"Someone obviously went to great lengths to create that musical combination lock."

Suddenly, the hologram uttered in a voice which was cracked with age; "Music is the universal language of all kind!"

"I have heard that somewhere before," mused Tom. "But isn't it '*mankind*'? I suppose it wouldn't be. Alienkind maybe..."

The figure gave a phlegmy cough and proceeded to sing out the combination, as Tom had, but several decibels louder. It coughed again.

"You're not keeping this combination much of a secret," said Tom. "If anyone hears you booming the solution then anyone will be able to break the code. Then again," Tom looked at the catastrophic mess which the pit had become and kicked some debris. "I suppose it's too late to worry about that now. And the combination wasn't exactly cryptic – to anyone with a glow rock to hand, anyway."

"Curiosity!" the hologram croaked. It was determined to utterly ignore the small human at its feet and insisted on staring ahead.

"Curiosity?"

"Curiosity is the gift which the founder of the truth beneath this building possesses."

"Er... do you mean me? I don't feel any the wiser. What *is* the truth? What is this place?"

"And truth you shall receive."

Can he even hear me? Is this just a recording?

"Curiosity!"

"Is this a recording on a loop?"

"Curiosity!"

"Yes, yes, I was curious," said Tom, impatiently. "Now can you indulge me in some answers? Unless…unless you want me to be *more* curious. Is that what you mean? Hmm…" Tom searched about him.

"I can't hear you."

"I suspected that," he murmured, sadly, but continued all the same. "Hmm... Is there a lever to pull, a switch to find or a box to open?" Tom searched through the rubble-filled pit in vain. "Or… or is it more of a question *of a question?* Do I simply need to ask the right questions?"

"Questions."

"And now you've turned into some kind of parrot!" Tom was losing patience. OK…well my question is… Who are you?"

"I am Professor Topica!"

"Finally!" whooped Tom. "Hello, Professor Topica."

"Of course!" he said, as though the thought had just

occurred to him. "I am the inventor of the Portal Re-router!"

CHAPTER 15

The grand ballroom, which once played host to summer dances and winter festivities of old, as well as modern opulent weddings was slowly filling up. Scores of indigo-skinned creatures filed into the room, occupying all manner of splendid seats borrowed from all corners of the great manor house. A raised platform occupied the area at the front of the room. There was much superficially civilised chatter as the attendees took their places and anticipated what was to follow. The setting sunbathed the grand room in a pink, dusky light which was fading fast. A young Radiakkan scurried across the room and experimented with the light switches. The first one he tried happened to activate an immense glitter ball which was positioned along a beam in the centre of the room. The pink sunlight reflected in the ball sparkled and shimmered in a polka dot pattern across the sea of invaders. Rather than getting up from their seats and dancing to *Come on Eileen,* however, the guests emitted a rumble of protesting grunts and barks.

"Apologies!" the unfortunate young Radiakkan cried out and proceeded to press all of the switches at once. Every single bulb in the room suddenly came on, gleaming brightly and flooding the room in light. Inopportunely, the glitter ball was now spinning at double speed and the audience was dazzled and bathed in pink, yellow and white polka dots. The grunting and barking swelled.

At the far side of the room, a luxurious purple floor-length curtain quivered in amusement.

"Stop laughing or we'll be caught!" Kayleesh whispered.

"I'm sorry," Nathan chortled. "But if they can't even operate a few light switches, how are they going to take over the planet?"

"This is serious. We don't want to end up like… like the Marquess and Marchioness!"

"I know, I know. I'll be quiet."

"And stop peeking out of the curtain – someone will spot us, Nathan. It's not worth the risk. We will be able to hear everything if we just *stay still.*"

"Well I hope no one performs a magic trick - I wouldn't want to miss that."

The grumbling and admonishments settled down as the glitter ball slowed and the lighting found a practicable level. Nathan heard a single pair of unhurried footsteps and the general chatter died down.

"Firstly, apologies for the rather unorthodox start to this very important gathering. Secondly, welcome to the new headquarters of Project Earth." A rumble of approval erupted through the room. The Radiakkans did not mark their appreciation with handclapping in the same way in which Earthlings would, but Nathan got the impression that their general tone and flapping of limbs indicated applause. "As some of you will already know, I am Nigel, the new Deputy Leader of this land. Our new Supreme Leader shall be taking to the stage shortly." A clamour of appreciation from the audience muffled the sniggers which arose behind the curtain at the reiteration of the Deputy Leader's name. "As all present company is purely Radiakkan, you may not all be aware of the fact that this building has been equipped with the latest ALSID equipment. This will make interrogation of undesirables simpler. This practice also reflects what has been fulfilled in other institutions. For example, hospitals and schools and other places the disgusting people of Earth deem to be important. Of course, the ALSIDs are not the only new systems to be put in place in these establishments, as our new Supreme Ruler will now explain. Project Earth participants, please welcome the Supreme Ruler of Radiakka II; *Jennifer.*"

"Are they serious?" Nathan whispered.

"Why shouldn't their leader be a female?" Kayleesh hissed.

The room escalated into sounds of approval and admiration and then the room fell silent. Nathan could almost taste the anticipation in the air. What sounded like a pair of high-heeled footsteps clip-clopped onto the stage. A swooshing of heavy robes and a light cough followed. Nathan restrained himself from peeking through the curtain. He could see that Kayleesh was curious too.

"I am delighted to see that every single one of the seats before me has been filled; filled with Radiakkan blood. This is what we need to see across the entire planet. The rotation I look around and see this on a grand scale is the rotation in which I shall be satisfied." A few cheers erupted. "I appreciate your enthusiasm, participants, but do keep silent until I have concluded my speech. I will then conduct a question and answer session, which will be a rare opportunity for us all to clarify things. Until then, please contain your voices."

"How civilised," whispered Nathan.

"That's because she's a woman." Kayleesh winked.

"As my deputy has mentioned, ALSIDs have already been placed to aid our takeover of this green planet. It is not a particularly convenient part of the plan, in fact it has been rather a hindrance, but nevertheless it has been a vital means of access to some of the higher establishments. Of course, the humans do not realise that they have been conversing through ALSID units, as they can be discreetly positioned in various locations. Secondly, they do not even remember their conversations with our many wonderful pherobots. So far, we have managed to keep our blue hands hidden from the general population with our methods and with the confusion of the pherofields. I would like to inform you of our progress with wiping out the humans. The plan has been going well so far – on a small scale.

"The Sickness has been spreading as our supply from Ronnus has been infiltrating the system. It is a long and slow process and we have not yet got enough to supply every city apartment, rural home or tribal village. However, thus far we have managed to populate the supply for mental institutions, breweries, cruise ships and some schools with our special liquid. We have recently received a substantial delivery from our supplier, and I am confident that that batch will be distributed over the course of the next few rotations.

"We do, however, have a problem in that the Earthlings have evidently started to notice a pattern. On their news programmes and across their communication networks they have begun to converse with each other on the matter of the Sickness which is becoming evident to them on the sea vessels and within the hospitals. It seems that this race is not as complacent and foolish as we suspected. Soon they may start to fight back!"

"She's not wrong!" spat Nathan.

"But if they do not know who they're fighting then this will prove difficult for them – we need to eradicate every single last one of them before they can retaliate!" Silence. "*Now* you can applaud!" Jennifer barked.

And applaud they did; whoops and cries and flapping of limbs filled the air. Nathan noticed that Kayleesh had pulled the curtain to one side slightly.

"She does look rather impressive," Kayleesh said. The audience were still making a commotion. "She is much more statuesque than the other Radiakkans. She's much more finely-dressed and has an air of dominance – it's kind of hard to describe."

"Then don't – I'll look myself." And Nathan did so. A proud, almost monumental, creature was strutting around the stage. Layers of rich clothing added to her prominence as she eyed her audience, a malicious grin dancing on her lips.

"Mute yourselves!" the Supreme Ruler bellowed. Her request was acted upon in an instant. "Now, who wishes to ask the first question?"

Nathan pushed the curtain back in place and the two of them remained silent as they listened.

"Supreme Ruler, while I am filled with admiration for your most respectable plans -"

"Enough of the false flattery and pathetic tones – we are Radiakkans, not Lymice! Speak with power and with my permission! Get on with it."

"Very well, Supreme Ruler. I know I am not alone here in thinking that the way in which we are going about Project Earth is too subtle. Many of us are wondering why we don't just blow the beggars up? Why poison the water supply and take lunar seasons to invade this planet, when we can make use of heavy artillery and eliminate the entire population within hours?"

"That is a worthwhile question, participant. Of course, the option has been discussed. But the simple matter is that we do not have enough weaponry to simply *eliminate the population within hours*. Plus, we would not want to risk destroying the landscape with highly destructive devices. We also do not want to risk alerting the planet's armed forces and trigger retaliation. If the inhabitants of this rock do not realise that they're being invaded, then they are not going to strike back as easily. From researching this planet, we have learned that not only do the humans have no knowledge of worlds beyond their own, but they are continuously occupying themselves in civil wars. If they're distracted by their petty wars between one small piece of green land and another small piece of green land, then they are less likely to make an alliance and fight another world with ease. It is only now that some of them are beginning to even notice the sickness and we have been here for several lunar seasons. You there – do you have our next question?"

"Are we going to make further use of the pherobots? I have not seen many on the streets of this land."

"The initial consignment of pherobots is currently working in hospitals as doctors, in schools as head teachers, in prisons as guards and in various other positions of authority. There are possible plans to ship over another consignment. They are magnificent, subtle tools of war and they serve us well. But they are not cheap."

"Are there any plans to roll out this plan further? Why not substitute the leaders of the nations with these marvels of engineering and control the humans that way?" the same voice inquired.

"Questions are restricted to one per participant; however, I shall overlook this rule in this instance. The Deputy Ruler and I have been in dialogue discussing such a scenario." Jennifer paused, seemed to suppress a sigh then continued. "However, we do not wish to make slaves of this race – we wish to eliminate them! We have neither room nor desire for humans to live amongst us – however useful they might be. In addition, a pherofield that large would be impracticable."

"Then why have the pherobots at all?" another voice asked. Nathan recognised it as the voice of the effeminate Radiakkan guard. The supreme leader considered the question for a few long moments before responding.

"Because the perfect mix of both methods of infiltration - the pherobots and the tainted water supply - is the optimum method of invasion. It is a two-pronged attack."

"But the pherobots don't necessarily attack, do they?" another participant piped up.

"Oh, they can do," Nigel piped up.

"And don't we know it?" whispered Nathan, rubbing his neck where the guard had grabbed him and remembering Kayleesh's collection of bruises.

"Are there any more questions before we adjourn?" the Supreme Ruler boomed.

"What is our next move, Supreme Ruler?"

"I'm glad that you asked, young participant. We have found army bases and groups of strong leaders across the continents. We need to infect these places next, as top priority!" an appreciative applause rippled through the rows. "And then… once the entire planet has been cleansed from human occupancy, we shall build up the institutions already in place and make Radiakka II inviolable and strong. After generations of hard work and once we've poured more and more capital into Project Earth, we shall appoint this planet our military base and take over the entire galaxy!"

CHAPTER 16

"I think we're out of our depth," Kayleesh sighed. She handed Nathan a bowl of steaming broth.

"*Now* you think we're out of our depth? We were barely treading water on arrival and now we're twenty thousand leagues under the sea!"

"We're what?"

"It doesn't matter. The *entire Galaxy?*" Nathan shuddered. "It's unbearable."

"We won't let it get that far. We can't." Kayleesh blew onto a spoonful of the hot soup. "At least we know what we're up against. Whether it's the whole planet or the whole galaxy under threat, we have to start small."

"With England?"

"With this building. Look, we're safe enough in here from the sickness. The water supply the Radiakkans have been using is not tainted." She supped a mouthful, by means of verification.

"How can we be safe? I have seen what happened to the Marquess and Marchioness… and to their poor little boy!"

"As long as we stick to the soup and fruit juice, we'll be safe." She tried to sound strong, but tears were forming in her eyes.

"So… that means that the water pitchers you brought up to the prisoners must have been contaminated. That's why I've been so sick!"

"Don't. I can barely even consider it! I'm so sorry Nathan. I didn't know that I was poisoning you!" she put down the bowl and hugged him. She was sobbing now.

"But why didn't you get ill too?"

"I didn't drink any of the water - I have had a taste for fruit juice ever since we visited your mother in the hospital." She pulled away and wiped her eyes on her sleeve.

"Mum!" Nathan cried out. "My Mum was drinking water by the glass full in the hospital. And Dad – he visited her there. He must have been poisoned there too. *He was so sick!*"

"How are *you* feeling?" Kayleesh sniffed. The whites of her eyes were damp and pink.

"Me? Oh… I am still feeling weak but maybe a combination of adrenalin and all this good soup has been helping my body combat the sickness."

"So there is a cure?"

"I think it's more of a preventative – simply stop drinking the poison! Hey – if that *is* the case then maybe my father is all right. Maybe now that he's home and drinking from the mainstream water supply he will have the chance to get well again!"

"Perhaps," said Kayleesh. And then added, earnestly, "but there is a chance that he had *too much* hospital tea in his system. He might be beyond the point of no return – he was not looking good. Besides, if we don't hurry, then the national water supply will be contaminated too. I'm sorry to be so blunt Nathan. But we need to act fast."

"But what do we do?"

"I have an idea." Kayleesh smiled. "But we'd better discuss it later. I can hear footsteps. Get inside the cupboard and we can discuss it tonight."

"The… the PR Machine?" Tom stammered.

Tom was not sure whether the hologram was responding to him directly or whether it was functioning as part of a system which relied on intelligent calculations. *Perhaps it has been set up to respond to predicted questions,* he thought. He pondered for a minute or two. What was the right way of conversing with this Professor Topica and what did he want to find out from him?

"Can you tell me why you are here?"

"Because my desire is for the truth to be uncovered -"

"But why hide it in the first place?"

"- I was the creator of the Portal Re-router. In turn I was the creator of this place," he continued.

"Crossvein Tourist Centre? Or do you mean Truxxe?"

"Truxxe; serendipitously so. And what a wonderful planet it is, so rich and full of life!" he croaked, in a voice more mature than an ancient cheese.

"Not without a few casualties," muttered Tom. His thoughts reverted back to when he learned of how the planet had been created. The Portal Re-router, Tom had learned in his previous adventures, had been designed to eliminate teleportation systems. The Luenians were a race who built up their economy on manufacturing and selling space crafts. Experimentation with teleports threatened the livelihood of Leuania. Therefore, the Luenians created the PR machine which interfered with teleportation systems and intercepted the paths of travellers. Instead of reaching their required destination, travellers were instead transported to the default position of Truxxe, along with a cumbersome chunk of whatever terrain the traveller happened to be standing on at the time. This process had fatal consequences and further trialling of teleportation was terminated. Consequently Truxxe, which was once a simple plain planetoid, became the amalgamation of many worlds. The planetoid was now rich in all manner of minerals and resources as an outcome of the interference caused by the PR machine.

The projection flickered a little.

"What is the truth?" asked Tom.

"The truth is that I, the creator of the Portal Re-router, did not wish for this to happen. I was commissioned the task of creating the device but when I found out the breadth of its devastating effects, I campaigned for it to be destroyed. But no one listened to me – the Luenian leaders were intent on keeping my protestations a secret and they continued to use the device I had invented."

Tom found it as difficult to have any anger for Professor Topica for his part in the invention of the PR, as he did for Einstein for his involvement in the atom bomb. But he was a little confused.

"So, what do you wish to gain from people knowing the truth? Do you want revenge? I know for a fact that the PR is no longer used, for I have seen it myself! The original machine is merely a trophy, kept on planet Leuania to remind the people there of their power."

"You have seen the Portal Re-router for yourself, truth-seeker?"

Tom nodded.

"The rotation has finally come."

"The rotation for revenge?"

"I do not seek revenge."

"I am glad of that. Then what is it you want? Do you want the Truxxians to be told that the creator of the PR machine was not the villain? Or do you want the Luenians to know the truth?"

"The Luenians know the truth. But they do not *wish* to know of it."

"Are you sure that you're really just a hologram? Can you really not hear me?"

"I can hear you, but not when you speak quietly."

"Oh, I see!"

"I am afraid that in my old age that my hearing has waned considerably." The great creature waggled a finger in his ear. He looked down at the human through black eyes.

"So, all this time, you have been responding directly to what I have been saying? Well… when you've been able to hear me of course," Tom said as loudly as her dared.

"My host may be telepathic, but I am not."

"Oh… so does that mean you're inside a -"

"- Speak up, truth seeker!"

"I'm sorry. Oh, and you can call me Tom!"

"Hello Tom, I am Professor Topica. Oh, I already told you that – my memory has also… weakened in recent decades… although not as much as my hearing."

"Please can you explain what you are doing here – how long have you been waiting?"

"Oh, I have been waiting for a long time. But not down here… I am actually at home, on planet Leuania, in my private holoceiver booth waiting for my lunch. I do wish my nephew would hurry up with my sandwiches…"

"You have your own holoceiver booth?"

"I was paid handsomely on completion of my invention. It was more of a bribe for my silence than payment, I fear." The old professor looked down, humbled and ashamed.

"But your holoceiver… it's so… it's huge!"

"It has been feeding off my contemplations and deliberations for many a year. I fear that I have over-fed it, rather. I have been waiting, you see. I have been waiting for such a rotation as this."

"But why?"

"I er… I actually forget. It has been so long. You triggered the programmed response with your choral combination which activated the auto-call back of my holoceiver. And… here we are."

"So I see. So… have you been waiting for help? Do you want to avenge the Luenians?"

"No… no… no Tom. I er… well, a bright young fellow like yourself… you have freed me from my time of er… waiting for… whatever it was I have been waiting for. What can I do for you?"

"What?" Tom paused for a moment. He was confused, fatigued and hungry and wished that he had eaten his bar snacks after all. He said sadly, "I don't think you'll be able to help me with my problems. They can't be solved by singing *do-re-mi* and activating a switch, unfortunately. And it's not a problem I could forget easily."

The hologram of the professor looked down at him, with pity in his eyes.

"Tell me, truth seeker Tom. What huge problem can ail the soul of such a tiny creature? But please, do remember to speak clearly and loudly for my old earholes."

"It's my home world, planet Earth. It's being invaded."

"Invaded? By whom? Not by the Lueanians?"

"No," Tom shook his head. "At least, I hope they're not involved too. In fact, I have no idea what is happening on

Earth right this moment, but I do know that it is under threat; by the Radiakkans."

"And why aren't you there, young Tom? Fighting or hiding or doing whatever must be done?"

"I *want* to be there, but I can't get there." Tom explained the whole story; Kayleesh and Nathan's premature voyage, the failed spotoon tour and how hopeless he felt about the whole matter. By the end of his account, Tom's throat was raw with having to speak so loudly and for so long. He questioned the benefit of spending so much energy and time talking to a being so far away – an elderly, slightly eccentric being at that. But in the absence of any alternative he decided to tell him everything. And he felt better for it.

"Your team came all the way back to Truxxe for a little two-wheeled one-person vehicle?"

"So it seems," Tom sighed. "You don't happen to have a vehicle, do you? In the way of a spaceship, perhaps? It doesn't have to be a very big one…"

Professor Topica paused for a moment before replying, "Me? No. No, I don't, sorry."

"That's all right," Tom sighed again. "It was worth a try. Maybe if I do some extra shifts at the Express Cuisine and get a night job –"

"- as a brain surgeon then you still won't be able to afford your own spaceship. Not before Earth has been pulverised into Radiakka II anyway."

"Then I'm out of options."

"Not necessarily, truth seeker Tom. You said that you had to rush back to Truxxe to retrieve your bicycle?"

Tom nodded.

"The Greys – when they first uncovered your bicycle – they thought that it might be dangerous, you say?"

"Well... it sounds silly, but I suppose they didn't know what it was. That was why Hyganty and Frarrk had to persuade them that it was harmless – or dormant at least. And then I was allowed to retrieve it."

"Hmm..." the old man pondered. "And why do you feel that you have to get to Earth?"

"Haven't you been listening? I need to get to my family, my friends, I need to stop –"

"- a whole race of malevolent creatures from taking over your world?" the professor interrupted him again. "One small boy, one big war. You may actually have an advantage by being here - on the outside!"

"I don't see how," Tom muttered, looking about the fragmented well.

"One person can achieve a lot – but they have to be in the right position to do it. I should know. Well I didn't know what my achievement would turn into, but the point is that you can make a difference."

"Can you invent me something rather quickly?" Tom asked, optimistically. "A huge ray gun the size of Mars to threaten them with might do!"

"You might have something there, truth seeker," the professor eyed him.

"Are you being serious?"

"We don't need an *actual* ray gun to be able to *threaten* them with a ray gun." Tom's hopes plunged as he realised that the old man's boat was sailing down senile river. "Let me explain." Tom did so, for he had little choice. He was stuck down a pit with a projection of a senescent old man who was waiting for his denture-friendly sandwich with its crusts cut off to be brought to him by his nephew. Or nurse. "If we threaten the Radiakkans – the original ones and probably the most important ones – who are living on Radiakka I, then they'll soon re-focus their efforts. We don't actually have to declare war, of course, we just need to make them think that they are under threat."

"It might work," said Tom. "Tell me more."

* * *

It was five o' clock in the morning and Nathan and Kayleesh were sitting in the kitchen of the manor house. The house was silent, save for the passing of the occasional pherobot guard. Kayleesh had napped on the bumpy makeshift bed which had been half-heartedly laid out for her by the Radiakkans in the corner of the kitchen. She had slept poorly but did not complain as she had at least had the luxury of a bed. Nathan had managed to seize a couple of hours of sleep, although a cupboard full of cleaning paraphernalia did not allow for the most comfortable repose. Kayleesh yawned as she dutifully sliced vegetables and meat for their captors' next meal. She hypothesised that not doing so would only arouse suspicion, plus it was difficult to rebel with the influence of the pherofield. She only hoped that the Radiakkans had forgotten about their prisoners, at least enough not to check whether they were still locked away in the servants' quarters. Or perhaps they assumed that they were now all dead. If Nathan had not escaped when he had, then he would almost certainly be. He realised that the invaders assumed that Nathan was dead, then they would not be actively looking for him.

"What was your idea, Kayleesh?" Nathan asked. He rubbed his back where a broom had been digging into his ribs. He was sure that he could feel an actual dent in his flesh. Kayleesh plopped a diced carrot into the large pot and picked up another. It was not the freshest of specimens, but she was not looking to enter Masterchef with this concoction.

"Yesterday evening, at the meeting, did you detect any unrest within the Radiakkans?"

"I noticed that they are a scheming, evil bunch of -"

"Did you notice any conflict of interest though?" Kayleesh interjected. "I am pretty sure that there might be a way to divide and conquer these parties."

"They all seemed to be on the same side to me – and they all want to take over the Earth!"

"True, but the Supreme Leader obviously wants to express her dominance. And I don't think that some of the male participants are comfortable with that - the Deputy in particular."

"But their race is so patriotic and proud – I thought that they worshipped their leaders!"

"Maybe, historically. But I definitely detected some discontentment in that room."

"So, what are you saying?"

"There are definitely cracks in the framework. I think that we can use any weakness to our advantage. And that might be a good place to start."

"So how do we communicate with them? We have already decided that we look too dissimilar to Radiakkans to emulate them and I am not sure that contacting the head office of the Daily Mail will work. Or would they be more likely to be Telegraph readers?"

"You might have something there, Nathan. Not about contacting the press – but we could release our own publication. That way we can keep it anonymous. Have you never heard of propaganda, Nathan?"

"It's a nice idea, but I'm not sure whether the Marquess and Marchioness would have owned their own printing press."

"No, but we don't need enough copies for an entire paper round. Half a dozen strategically placed items of literature might suffice."

"So perhaps the pen can be mightier than the sword!"

"I'm not sure what you mean by that, but I think that it's worth a try. I'll go in search of some stationery and we'll get started."

There was apparently a problem with the Cluock II. Schlomm and Hannond Putt had aversely landed just off the M5 motorway. The supply ship was nestled in a thick coppice which was concealed from the passing traffic. More accurately, it was nestled in muddy bog water. And not so much nestled, as stuck fast. While Schlomm ranted and grunted as he paced the decks of the malfunctioning ship, a passer-by who was walking his schnauzer, gave a fleeting glance at the mud-spattered spacecraft. The schnauzer sniffed the ground around the bog and whimpered at the unreachable anomaly. The man pulled back on his lead, to prevent it from venturing through the mud. It was cold and dark, and the man wanted to get home to his family. He was not interested in investigating a mound of filthy metal. Besides, he had not felt well since his meal at the pub that afternoon and was having a difficult time preventing himself from vomiting. He retched, and clamped his hand over his mouth, for the stench of the swamp was not helping matters. He pulled the reluctant pooch away and vowed never to order the salmon again.

The Cluock II was planted at an angle in the mud so Hannond had a job to traverse the ramp as he got off the ship. His jumped down and his flat feet splattered into the muddy water and he waded to the grassy shore. He sniffed the air.

"The air is sweet," he said to himself. "It reminds me of Glorb."

Schlomm shortly followed him and the two Glorbians stood in the thicket, now almost indistinguishable from one another, with their matted, dank hairy bodies.

"We need an engineer. And possibly a crane," Hannond observed.

"I need a burger," Schlomm grumbled. He squelched off in the direction of a set of distant bright lights. Hannond followed him.

The hologram of Professor Topica, who was only slightly more hard-of-hearing than he was eccentric, elaborated on his idea to threaten the Radiakkan invaders. He told Tom of a machine which he had been working on for more than a decade. But the professor had tinkered and toyed with the machine so long, and between so many other projects, that he had forgotten its original intention.

"I don't know what one quarter of the parts even *are* any more," he said in dismay. "And I think that the parts that are still missing are now obsolete! If I don't know what it's supposed to do then I doubt anyone else would. My Nephew found it in my work shed a few weeks ago and thought that it was some kind of bomb! He did have a terrible fright. I had to explain to him that it wasn't a bomb... but that I didn't know what it was intended to be... quite embarrassing really. Anyway... my point is... that if it *looks* like a weapon already, then with some additions of some offensive-looking embellishments, it could be a work of art! Or at least a fake weapon." The professor continued. "So, if we can get the message across to the Radiakkans that we have the intention of deploying the... er... weapon... then they may surrender!"

"I think I understand," said Tom. "But how do we get the weapon to Radiakka if neither of us has a ship?"

"I am the inventor of the PR and I know how the teleporter works. I do have one in the back of my shed. It'd probably be good for one more use. I wouldn't recommend using it for organic matter transportation. But for an inanimate object on the other hand..."

"An inanimate object such as a device which looks like a weapon..."

"Exactly!"

Tom grinned.

"So, young Tom, do you know the address of the building?"

"No, but I know someone who does."

CHAPTER 17

Gracer Menille responded to Tom's call through his timepiece and gave the exact position of the place where she used to work, so that the professor's holoceiver could locate the grounds of the Wheylandian Parliamentary building.

"Why do you need to know, Tom? What are you doing and where are you?"

"I'm at Crossvein Tourism Centre," he told her.

"What are you doing there? Is it even open at this time of night?"

"It's all rather complicated to explain... but I will probably need to finish what I started before the museum opens again... because the staff really won't be happy with the state of their floor."

"What are you talking about? What have you done?"

"Just trust me. I think I have a way of saving the Earth."

"That's fantastic news! All by yourself?"

"Not exactly. Look... just stay nearby in case I need you. You and Raphyl and the others. Just stay safe at TSS. I'll contact you tomorrow."

"Are you talking to your girlfriend?" The professor's hologram appeared before him once more.

"No... I can't seem to be able to contact her via my timepiece. I think there might be a problem with hers," he said, glumly. And then mumbled, sadly, "I really hope that she's all right."

"What was that, Tom? You will need to speak up."

"It doesn't matter," he said. "Have you been working on the weapon?"

"I have indeed. I am afraid that it does not look as good as I would have liked..." The huge depiction of Professor Topica said, a little deflated. "I would have liked another two or three years to work on it. But, from the panic in your eyes, I see that we do not have another two or three years. So, three hours will have to suffice."

"So, what do we do next?"

"Do you wish to see the 'weapon'?"

"Of course!"

"Then bear with me while I disconnect and retrieve the machine." The professor's hologram faded.

Schlomm Putt squinted in the dark night and looked up at the incandescent lettering above a glass double door.

"I can't make out what it says, Hannond." He grumbled.

"Perhaps there isn't an ALSID in this building," Hannond shrugged.

"Primitive race," Schlomm spat. "Well I can smell grilled meat of some description. Let's go inside." They passed through the automatic sliding glass doors and into the warm interior of the motorway service station.

"But how will they be able to understand us? I don't speak human."

"I'm not looking for a conversation with these creatures. I just want a burger."

"But we'll have to pay for one! How will we order?"

Schlomm spun around and said, angrily, "Hannond, we're meat delivery specialists. If we hadn't used all of the available storage space on the Cluock II for those barrels, then we would have a ship full of the stuff. I can't bring myself to part with remuneration for one measly burger."

"You have a point. Hey, that man has one!" Hannond pointed at a teenage boy, cap pushed down over his eyes, headphones blaring into his ears, chomping on a greasy hamburger as he walked towards the exit. Schlomm licked his lips and tugged at the boy's jeans, instantly dirtying them with his grimy grip.

"Give that to me."

The teenager, keen to exit the service station and be on his way, shook his leg in an attempt to free it from the Glorbian. He complained through a mouth full of food, "Gerroff, you crazy mutt!"

"I demand it! I need sustenance!"

"I said, get off me, you filthy freak!" he mumbled, and a blob of barbeque sauce plopped from his mouth and landed on Schlomm's face. Schlomm lost his grasp on the boy's leg and one final kick sent the Glorbian skidding across the shiny floor. Hannond sniffed the substance on Schlomm's face and watched as he licked the sauce from his matted fur. Schlomm smiled in approval.

The teenager straightened his jeans to the best of his ability, cursed under his breath and turned up the volume on his Walkman.

"If I could be bothered, I would go and find your owner and ask him to buy me a new pair of jeans!" He shouted in Schlomm's direction and trudged through the sliding doors.

"I wonder what he said," pondered Hannond.

"We need to find a burger that's not attached to an Earthling. Preferably one covered in that very tasty sauce."

"Earthlings in barbecue sauce? That doesn't sound very appetising."

The double doors opened again, and an elderly lady stumbled in, clutching her stomach. She spotted a sign directing customers towards the toilet facilities but stopped just short of the entrance and promptly vomited all over her plimsolls.

Schlomm scratched his backside and let out a noxious belch. "No, Hannond, I wouldn't want to eat a human. They really are disgusting creatures."

Kayleesh and Nathan had fashioned booklets from notepaper and found half a dozen ball-point pens which were in the kitchen's recipe drawer. Kayleesh already had pen to paper and gave the impression of a keen student embarking on a school project. Nathan was doing a perfect impersonation of himself as a school pupil and was staring at a blank page.

"I have no idea what to write," he sighed. "Tom would know exactly what to put."

"We need to create some controversy," Kayleesh said simply. "I'm writing an article about how female rulers are unnatural with weak laws and that the very idea of them undermines the strength of the Radiakkan empire."

"Is that right?"

"Of course it isn't – in fact I'm finding it rather a challenge to write from this point of view – but we need to sway their thoughts and if this is what they're already thinking then reading it for themselves in black and white will affirm their views."

"If you say so," said Nathan. "OK, I'll leave the articles to you. How about I draw a cartoon of Jennifer? She could be giving out glasses of poisoned water to humans who are dying one at a time. And in the next frame I'll draw pherobot rulers attacking people by the hundred. And maybe add some kind of caption which asserts that the Supreme Ruler's ways are wrong, and that the Deputy Rulers are right."

"You're a genius, Nathan!"

He grinned. "Teamwork."

The hours passed as the two worked on their collaboration; Kayleesh with her controversial deliberations and Nathan with his drawings. After their project was completed, they began work on several copies of the publication, which was time-consuming, but they both agreed that one copy would have little impact. When the sun rose and it was time for Kayleesh to serve breakfast to her captors, Nathan sat in the cupboard, hiding and continuing with his work. He remained there for the bulk of the day while Kayleesh split her time between writing and meal preparation. They kept their strength up with bowls of chunky soup and it was soon night-time again.

It was well into the early hours when they compiled their work. They were so tired that they had little energy to talk at length. They managed to gather their strength enough to dodge the pherobot guards and distribute their handiwork as far as their courage would allow. Then they wearily returned to the kitchen and took to their respective sleeping areas.

Three short hours later, Nathan was woken by the sound of Kayleesh preparing steaming soup for the Radiakkans' breakfast. An idea occurred to Nathan. He didn't know why he had not thought of it before.

"Kayleesh," he said, closing the cupboard door behind him and peering into the soup pot. "Why don't we play the Radiakkans at their own game?"

"What do you mean?"

"Well, they're poisoning us, so why don't we poison them?"

"I did think of that," she said, balancing a tower of breakfast trays. "But on my first morning here I discovered that they have employed one of their minions as a food taster, and if poisoned food harmed him then I am sure that my actions would not go unpunished. Besides, I didn't want to risk contaminating my own meals. I'm getting a little bored of the same old food, but it's better than the alternative."

"I see," said Nathan, a little dismayed. "Well I just hope that our little campaign works."

"So, do I. You should hide away again while I circulate the breakfast things. I'll let you know if I hear of any turbulence amongst the Radiakkans."

Nathan nodded, but did not go back to his hiding place straight away. A pherobot had not long passed the door so he took the opportunity to stretch his aching muscles. He was not used to such a cramped sleeping space. It felt good to ease his tender shoulder muscles, crick his neck and click his joints back into place. He paced around the kitchen, loosening up his limbs. His thoughts turned to Tom. He wondered whether he had managed to follow them to Earth. And if he had returned home, then where was he now? Had he and the others managed to figure out that it was the water supply that was making the humans sick and had they managed to avoid getting sick themselves? Had he been trying to contact Kayleesh on his timepiece like she had with him?

He shuddered at the idea of his friend suffering the same fate as the prisoners in the mansion, and the same fate as his family. He cursed himself for having not been firmer with his mother. He should have taken her with him and freed her from that toxic place. Perhaps he could call the hospital. He could ring and check whether she was all right. But would Doctor Byrne be truthful with him? Would he even let him speak to her? Also, the plan would involve having access to a telephone, which he did not have. He felt so helpless. He stopped suddenly, as he heard voices crescendo as they passed along the corridor.

"I'd like to know who had a hand in writing this," one of them barked.

"It is the work of a genius!" the other exclaimed. Nathan hid behind the door, for he feared that the conversation would be out of earshot if he took sanctuary in the cupboard. "It simply says what we've all been thinking," the second voice continued.

"Exactly! I wouldn't dare to utter anything like this in the presence of the Supreme Ruler, or air my views on paper, but someone has obviously had the gall!"

"It is certainly proof that we're not alone in our disdain of her methods. We need stronger ways in which to eradicate this planet of its vermin human population. *And a pitiable female so-called leader is not the man for the job!*"

"Are you certain that you did not produce this document?" There was a rustling of paper.

"Absolutely certain! I would have been proud to have produced it and would have told you had I created such a marvellous publication!"

"I am certain that you would have, brother. I wonder who *did* produce it."

"I don't see that it matters all that much, ultimately," the voice scoffed. "Let's see if we can find anyone else who agrees with it, before all of the participants vacate the headquarters and go on their way."

"We can't ask anyone directly," the other warned. "There are still those who do support the Supreme Ruler.

We should be reprimanded if we show any signs of discontent to her immediate supporters."

"You have a point. However, from the meeting two Earth rotations ago, I don't think Jennifer has even the support of the Deputy Ruler."

"Then we shall seek him and discuss the publication with him!" The voices faded as they passed along the corridor. Nathan grinned to himself.

Tom Bowler had been waiting for over an hour for the professor's return. He was beginning to panic. He was relying on the senile old Luenian to help him save his planet and he was running out of time. What was he doing that was taking him so long? How far did he have to transport the device to the holoceiver and why had he left the booth anyway? He knew from his experience at TSS that the psychic creatures were not confined to their booths. He wondered whether the old man had been in the booth for so long that he had lost his way in his own house.

Maybe the old coot has croaked and hasn't even made it as far as the device, he wondered. He waited a while and was conscious that it was the early hours of the morning. *I can't wait down here indefinitely. I am going to get caught. Maybe I should check that no staff have arrived yet to open up.*

Tom waved the glow rock around the pit, and the illumination fell upon the fallen railing. He jerked the railing so that it swivelled to a ninety-degree angle and the rails had the function of ladder rungs. He was rather pleased with himself as he placed a foot on the bottom rung and began to climb out of the pit. He was almost at the top when a light flickered behind him and a voice suddenly boomed.

"Where do you think you're going?"

Tom nearly fell off the railing, in surprise. He climbed back down into the pit to face the hologram of professor Topica once more.

"I apologise for the delay," the giant hologram announced. Large eyes regarded him.

"I was beginning to wonder what had happened to you," Tom grumbled.

"My nephew had made a plateful of sandwiches and I stopped by the dining room to eat lunch with him for the first time in a very long time!"

"What?" Tom stared, open-mouthed. He was infuriated. "That's what you were doing all that time - *eating sandwiches?"*

"They were particularly nice sandwiches – Augtopian cheese and traditional Luenian pickle." The Professor appeared to be licking his lips.

"I don't care if they're Glorbian caviar and mustard!" Tom shouted.

"What? Oh dear, that would never do. Glorbian caviar is not something one should ever put on a sandwich – or, indeed, put in one's mouth." The Luenian made a face filled with disgust. Tom sighed.

"Do you at least have the device?"

"The what?"

"The weapon!"

"Weapon? I don't own any weapons."

"You said that you were going to get the device you'd been working on – the fake weapon. Then we were going to threaten the Radiakkan government!"

"We were?"

Tom nodded, vigorously. "I have the address."

"Well done boy! Well... er... let me go and get it then."

Kayleesh returned from her duties and pulled open the kitchen cupboard door in excitement.

"I think our plan is working!" she exclaimed.

"Please knock next time!" said Nathan. He had his back to the door and was urinating in a mop bucket.

"Nathan!" Kayleesh yelled and shut the door again.

"You're the one who walked in unannounced!" Nathan shouted through the door. "It's not as though I'm peeing into the soup. There's not much choice of suitable receptacle back here!" When Nathan appeared again he washed his hands in the kitchen sink and dried them on his clothes. He sniffed his hands.

"What are you doing?" asked Kayleesh.

"I'm seeing if I can smell poison on my hands after washing them in the water."

"I see. Don't put them near your mouth just in case. Anyway, as I was saying, while I was walking around the manor, I have heard many whisperings about our handiwork!"

"As have I!" said Nathan and told her about the conversation he had heard. Kayleesh grinned.

"It seems that news has travelled quickly!"

"Has everyone that *you* have heard discussing the publication been in favour of it too?"

"Not all, no. But that doesn't matter. In fact, that's a good thing. It makes the Supreme Ruler's supporters uncomfortable to know that there is a counter group."

"Very true. Divide and conquer!"

"That is the idea," she said and giggled.

"So, what do we do next?"

"We go back to our second home – behind the curtain in the ballroom. There's an emergency meeting taking place this very afternoon!"

"Well the curtain is a welcome break from the cupboard."

CHAPTER 18

"We have had word from the homeland!" The Supreme Ruler announced. She spoke with extra transcendence, as though verifying her leadership status. But there were undertones of fear in her voice. A few moments of murmuring from the audience followed. Nathan and Kayleesh looked at each other and mouthed *the homeland?* For they were both expecting a discourse on their propaganda pieces. "It seems that our beautiful planet Radiakka is being threatened!" Louder murmuring ensued. "You hear correctly, participants. An enemy is threatening to attack Radiakka I and annihilate our rulers at the Wheylandian Parliamentary Building if we do not cease with Project Earth. In point of fact there is a presently a deadly weapon in close proximity to the building!"

"How could this have happened?" a participant called out. "We were told that Earthlings would not have the technology nor the means to make actions such as this."

"It is possible that knowledge of the invasion has leaked out, that the humans have found allies beyond their solar system. The message received by the perpetrator cannot be traced. But we cannot take these threats lightly."

"Are you saying that we have to hold fire?" It was Nigel's voice.

"We have little choice, Deputy." A leering tone and a swish of her robe followed.

"But we're behind schedule already – we should have eliminated all of the Earthlings by now! I *knew* that the two-pronged method would never work. It's too late – they're already fighting back!"

"Such panic in your voice!" Jennifer sounded enraged. "Such lack of control – these are not the qualities of a Deputy Leader!"

And then something unexpected happened. The sound of a shooting laser, followed by a sickening crack, the crumple of a body falling to the floor and an almost instantaneous odour of burning flesh. Kayleesh and Nathan gasped, each fighting for the edge of the curtain to peak at the events unfurling on stage. At Jennifer's feet lay the smouldering body of Nigel, the Deputy Leader. The audience appeared to be as stunned as they were as Jennifer concealed her weapon within her robes. There was the scraping of a few chairs as participants attempted to stand or leave, but otherwise no sound as no one dared to speak. All eyes were on the corpse of the expired Deputy.

"Let that be a lesson to all of you doubters and unbelievers!" Jennifer bellowed. She swished her robe about her as she paraded around, her heels click clacking about the stage. "And don't think that I don't know about the little newspapers that many of you have been passing around this morning. That's right *I know.*"

Kayleesh looked at Nathan as they cowered behind the curtain once more.

What have we got ourselves into? Nathan thought.

"When I find out who started that little antic, they will soon regret ever putting pen to paper or ever breathing the same air as I! But I do thank the creator of such a disgusting piece of *journalism* in one respect," she spat, "for without such I would not have learned of the true spirit of so many of you, so-called, participants! There is no room for any of you insubordinate creatures in this room!"

Next came the sound of three more shots as the Supreme Leader disclosed her weapon once more. Nathan and Kayleesh did not dare to look this time as they heard the sound of three more bodies hit the floor and the gasps of the onlookers. The two of them sat shaking and pale behind the curtain.

"Please – don't shoot!" a voice from the audience wavered. "I just want to know what our next move is. I am not one of the unbelievers – your way is the right way! Tell us your next move. Tell us what we must do next."

"Now *that* is the right spirit. But *stop cowering and act like a true Radiakkan!*"

"She's crazy!" Nathan whispered. Kayleesh nodded.

"We cannot continue with Project Earth while our homeland is under threat. We must retreat and return to Radiakka where we are strong!" another voice called out.

"But what about Project Earth?" called another.

Another laser shot. The stench of burning flesh.

"You're shooting even your true followers now! You're insane!" a female participant yelled. "You're not in control at all – you can't even convince yourself of that fact!" A laser shot, followed by another panicked laser shot and another, interspersed with the sound of running footsteps. But the sound of her body crumpling to the floor indicated that the female Radiakkan had not managed to escape.

Kayleesh and Nathan could not resist finally looking out from behind the curtain at the lunacy which was taking place before them. The Supreme Leader, insanity in her eyes, had stepped down from the stage, and was waving her weapon around haphazardly. She pointed her gun at the young Radiakkan who had struggled with the lighting system at the previous meeting and shot him dead. The participants, apparently angered by the gratuitous murder of the youngster, were now all upstanding and appeared to be descending on her.

"Guards!" Jennifer hollered. "Rid me of this unrelenting psychopathy!"

"She's flipped!" Nathan said, wide eyed. "Discovering that she is scorned by her own people has sent her over the edge!"

"So, it seems – plus she just learned that Radiakka is in danger. I wonder if that is really true. Could it be anything to do with Tom?"

"Of course it is!" Nathan grinned. "Who else is clever enough to have got involved with something so ingenious?"

"You could be right – I wonder how he did it though – I wonder who he has an alliance with?"

"The Truxxians maybe, or the Submians?"

"I can't wait to ask him and find out," grinned Kayleesh, suddenly feeling more positive.

"If we ever get out of here alive," said Nathan. "Hey look!" He nodded towards the furore. The Supreme Leader was pointing her weapon at a petrified Radiakkan, but it appeared to be malfunctioning. The Radiakkan's relief was short-lived, however, as a trio of pherobot guards advanced into the room and began to attack the participants one by one. Kayleesh and Nathan gripped the edge of the material until their knuckles almost burst through their skin. Their hearts thumped loudly, their eyes darting about the room, taking in the entire event. They hoped that they would not be spotted but both seemed powerless to move – they were utterly frozen in fear. The pherobots proceeded to grasp each Radiakkan by the neck and terminate them with ease until the only indigo-skinned creature left standing was the Supreme Leader.

Nathan half-expected her to give an evil cackle or at least a triumphant smirk, but instead she slumped to the floor. She remained there, and Nathan realised that she was actually weeping.

Then she began to wail.

"Why? *Whyyyyyyyyyyyyyy?*"

Nathan and Kayleesh looked at each other.

One of the pherobots let the body of his last victim drop to the floor. A second later his camera lens turned to the curtain. Kayleesh and Nathan tucked quickly behind it, but it was too late.

The pherobot guard's lens focused in on the curtain. The two other guards focused their lenses too. It was the single most terrifying sound that Nathan had ever heard.

As the guards advanced towards where they were hiding, the strength of the pherofield was too strong to resist.

Compliantly, Nathan and Kayleesh came out from behind the curtain.

Kayleesh and Nathan stood before the pherobot guards and before the Supreme Leader; a leader who had annihilated all of her subjects. She stood up and waved the malfunctioning weapon at the two of them.

"Who... who are you... and what were you doing in this top-secret meeting?"

The guards continued to advance.

"Halt! I need to converse with these creatures before you destroy them." The guards did as they were commanded and stopped dead.

Kayleesh was visibly shaking, but she took a step forward and a very deep breath.

"Kayleesh and Nathan; Augtopian and Earthling. We are here to end this."

"Prisoners... prisoners, both of you," Jennifer wavered.

"That's what we wanted you to think," Kayleesh said. "But we knew what we were doing. Who would have thought that one little publication would have caused the destruction of your little *project?*"

"You... it was *you?*" Jennifer unconsciously lowered her laser gun. "Don't be under the misapprehension that you are responsible for this – two pathetic creatures like yourselves. There is more to the demise of the participants!"

"Well, your gun had a lot to do with it!" chipped in Nathan. "Or do you mean... *The deadly weapon*?"

"You know about the *weapon?"*

"Of course! We know exactly what will happen if you do not retreat," Kayleesh falsified. "Remove all of your minions from this planet or it shall be deployed with immediate effect! Rid this green Earth of your armies, your poisoned water and your loathsome pherobots and leave this planet alone."

Nathan swelled with pride at his friend's bravery and intelligence.

"Do you really think that it's going to be that simple to stop me?" Jennifer threw down her weapon and thrust her hands into the air. "Guards! Destroy the two prisoners!"

CHAPTER 19

The human and Augtopian gasped as the image of Tom Bowler flickered into being before the Supreme Leader. He turned away from the startled Radiakkan to look at his friends and watched helplessly as the guards descended upon them. One of them began to encircle his girlfriend's neck with his cold, strong, bronze hands. Tom screamed out, waving his arms fruitlessly, his projection simply falling through metal.

"Stop! STOP!"

And the guards stopped dead.

Kayleesh gulped.

Nathan helped her out of the grasp of the statue-like pherobot and the two of them stared at Tom.

"How did you do that?" asked Nathan.

"I... I don't know."

"Oh, come on now, you don't think *he* did this do you?" Jennifer huffed.

"Well how else do you explain it? Your guards have all been disabled!"

"Purely coincidental," said Jennifer. "The guards have run out of charge, and unfortunately, so has my weapon. On arrival we discovered that this backwards planet does not possess universal charge points."

"What?" Nathan and Tom could not help but laugh.

"This occurrence was inevitable. I just didn't think it would be so soon – the shipment of universal chargers was due with the next consignment of pherobots." She shouted out in frustration.

"So, all of the guards are now disabled – world-wide?" Nathan asked.

"So it would seem." The Supreme Leader stood with slumped shoulders. Her weapon useless, her guards mere statues and her subjects all destroyed.

"The threat still stands. The weapon shall be deployed if you don't retreat," said Kayleesh.

"How did you..." Tom began. And then he grinned. It had all come together perfectly. Although he had wanted to have been the one to give the Supreme Leader the news. This seemed to happen to him a lot. "She's right," he said. "And the weapon is very deadly indeed. It could take out your entire population with the flick of a switch. And we have more of them on standby."

"Ah, your trump card," Jennifer spat.

Just as Nathan was beginning to relax, a sudden stirring from the corner of his vision startled him.

"Er bud... I don't think it's over yet."

Tom watched, helplessly as one of the guards burst into life and made for Kayleesh. Its crudely cut, metallic face was somehow filled with malice. Kayleesh shrieked and flailed her arms, much to Jennifer's delight. Nathan lunged forwards to her aid, but Jennifer grabbed his arms and the tall Radiakkan clamped him to the spot. The guard's cold, hard hands were now upon the Augtopian and Tom begged the android to stop, hoping that the success of his previous protestations were not just coincidence. He yelled at the guard and he yelled at Jennifer. He looked on in horror as both Kayleesh and Nathan wriggled in the arms of their captors.

The guard seemed to be losing power once more and his grip was loosening. Nathan mustered up all of his remaining strength and kicked his foot backwards into the body of the Radiakkan, simultaneously biting down on her arm and screaming out some kind of maddening war cry. The shocked Jennifer, clearly having had the breath kicked out of her, slumped to the ground, her grasping hands scraping the floor and grappling for purchase on Nathan's ankles. But he was already at Kayleesh's side, prising the weakened guard's limbs from Kayleesh's body. With one final growl he tore the guard away from her, and kicked the robot's left leg, causing it to falter and crash to the floor.

It lay still. Unmoving.

Nathan stood panting, then held his friend in an embrace of relief. She was shaking but unhurt.

"I think it's time for me to retire," Jennifer croaked. "I was never cut out for this. I was class president at school, leader of one of the great parties in Wheyland at sixteen – but this... this is just too much. I can't take over one paltry planet, let alone an entire galaxy. Have your precious water supply back. Trade in these heaps of metal for cash. I no longer care for such things!" Jennifer stumbled ungracefully to her feet, pulling off her heels. She nursed her arm which was bleeding from Nathan's hefty bite. "Yes, that's right... I'll retire... I'll live in a simple dwelling by a pink lake on a distant planet. Maybe I'll breed flopula rodents and grow my own vegetables." Her eyes were distant, as though she was already in some faraway land.

"She really has cracked!" said Nathan.

Jennifer let her robes drop to the floor and was soon standing in the middle of the ballroom, barefooted and in a simple hand-woven dress. She pattered across the floor and out of the ballroom. Nathan, Kayleesh and Tom's hologram ran after her. They followed her along the corridor, through a door out into the courtyard. She stopped suddenly and stooped to pick a conker from the ground. She rubbed it's smooth, brown surface between her hands."

"Such a beautiful fruit. Why should your shell be so spiky?"

They watched, open-mouthed, as Jennifer wandered across the courtyard and began to ascend invisible steps. She put out a hand and opened an invisible door and soon she was gone. The cloaked ship made its presence known with a horrendous roaring of engines. Nearby plant life waved and rustled as the ship apparently launched itself into the cosmos.

"The crazy woman turned into a hippy!" gasped Tom.

"If she's going to be a hippy she'll have to get rid of that spaceship," Nathan waved at the fume-filled air and spluttered.

"Tom! I'm so glad that you're all right. I wish I could hug you!" said Kayleesh.

"I'm sure you'll be able to soon enough," said Nathan. Let's get back to the train station and get back to the ship.

"But Nathan," said Kayleesh. "Don't you want to go home and see your Dad?"

"I... I don't know if I can. I have kind of accepted that neither of my parents are alive."

"You don't know that. And what about Tom's parents? You can't just leave!"

"But I need to get you home, Kayleesh. I need to get you back to Tom!"

"No, wait there – I'll come for you," said Tom. His image was starting to fade. "Wait for me at your house."

It was a long walk back to Nathan's neighbourhood. He expected that they could have sought out a bus stop, but the walk refreshed them. They were both in shock and the fresh air and cool breeze was a welcome change from the stuffy kitchen of the manor house.

"I can't believe that Tom came back!" Kayleesh said for the fifth time. "Do you think that he was using the holoceiver booth at TSS?"

"If they've managed to employ a new one of those holoceiver creatures, then I suppose that that was where he was calling us from."

"How is he going to get to Earth and meet up with us? His call didn't last very long, and I had so many things I wanted to ask him," said Kayleesh.

"Same here. At least we know he's alive and well though. And he knows that we're all right too." Kayleesh nodded, thoughtfully. Nathan added, "I just hope my father is."

Nathan let them into the house. He ran up the stairs and straight into his parent's bedroom. The bed was empty. He called out.

"I'm down here, Nathan." Nathan scooted back down the stairs and he and Kayleesh found his father tidying up the kitchen. Nathan wasn't sure what surprised him most – the fact that he was very much alive and looking healthier than he had done in years or the fact that he had a dishcloth in his hand.

"Dad!" He gave his father a huge hug. "You're... you're well!"

"Yes, yes, *I'm* quite well." Nathan noticed a sadness in his father's eyes. A lump formed in his throat as he reached for the breakfast bar stool behind him and slowly sat down. He opened his mouth to ask the worst question he could ever think of asking, but his brain could not let him do it. Nathan's question was answered, however, and he found himself clasping his hands over his ears, as though blocking out what his father was telling him would somehow stop it being true. He read his father's lips before closing his eyes and blocking out his vision too.

"I'm so sorry, Nathan. But your mother... your mother passed away."

No, no, no!" Nathan screeched. Kayleesh enveloped him in a comforting embrace as he sobbed. He could hear her softly saying "Poor Carol," over and over.

The next hour passed by in a blur of surreality. He knew the truth; he knew that the reason his mother was dead was that the Radiakkans had succeeded in poisoning her; poisoning her body and poisoning her mind with sullied water and the constant confusion of pherofields. But the fact that his mother had been a casualty of the planned Radiakkan invasion seemed to be unknown to his father.

His version of events, through rolling tears, was that the doctors had not been able to save her, that she had been too weak to fight the Sickness. Nathan was too choked to contradict him, and Kayleesh didn't correct him either. The three of them simply wept. His father continued to talk about his wife's deterioration, but the words washed over him. The awful truth just wouldn't settle; his mind would not yet wholly accept it.

And then another thought occurred to him.

"How come you're all right Dad? I'm so relieved you are well, but last time we saw you -"

"- I eventually fought off that stomach bug I was suffering with. It hung around for quite a while but after a few days of a diet of plain water and rest I was soon back on my feet, thankfully."

Nathan wasn't so sure that a stomach bug had been the culprit. For he had, himself, been poisoned and had recovered. But it didn't matter now. All that mattered was that his father had survived. He had gone back to drinking ordinary water, since leaving the hospital, and his body had had the chance to recuperate. He only wished his mother had had the same chance.

"Tom's parents – are they all right? And his cousin Max and -"

"Nathan, Nathan, everyone else is fine," he reassured his son. "They are all as shocked as we are about your mum's death, but everyone will be fine."

"No, I didn't mean -"

"Why don't you two go and sit in the lounge and I'll put the kettle on?"

Nathan wiped his eyes and nodded.

As they sat, clutching warm mugs of tea, the start of the six
o' clock news chimed on the television. Kayleesh prodded Nathan and he looked up at the screen. A reporter was speaking over footage of Trafalgar Square where what appeared to be statues were standing in the middle of the street.

"The bronze sculptures have seemingly appeared overnight with no explanation. The statues have been spotted in cities, parks, offices, schools and hospitals country wide. Reports are also coming in from overseas of similar occurrences. Just what are these statues and where did they come from? Why did no one notice them arrive? Are they part of some elaborate student prank or the work of a wealthy installation artist? There will be more updates as the investigation proceeds." Nathan and Kayleesh looked at each other. "In other news, the Sickness epidemic which has affected isolated regions, seems to be coming to an end. Fewer cases have been reported and some are even recovering. More details later in the programme." Nathan smiled, although resentment for his mother's fate burned deep and he knew that it always would. The journalist continued, "our other main story is that communication issues of a very unusual nature have swept the nation. Scientists are baffled as language barriers have been almost completely lifted as citizens are suddenly able to understand one another. Whatever has caused this perplexing occurrence may seem serendipitous, but the phenomenon has caused confusion and chaos in the nation's schools. Teachers of French, German, Spanish and Cantonese have been caught up in the confusion as one hundred percent of pupils are now achieving A grades.

Nathan and Kayleesh almost covered the freshly cleaned carpet in tea as they exploded into laughter.

It had been over a week since Nathan had returned home. Kayleesh had been staying in the guest room and the two of them had regained their strength with a proper varied diet and plenty of rest. The funeral had come and gone and the news items on the television and tabloids were as wild as ever. Speculations of the reasons for the planet's recent unorthodox events never once touched on the truth and it became apparent that the two friends were the only ones on the planet who knew what had really happened. Nathan had thought that perhaps he would tell the authorities what really happened and how close the world had been to a total invasion. But he had seen enough of the inside of psychiatric hospitals to last him a lifetime.

It was a Sunday afternoon when Nathan opened the door to find Tom standing on the doorstep. Kayleesh flew past Nathan and threw her arms around him. Tears of joy ran down her face and they locked in a long-awaited embrace.

"Come in!" Nathan said, grinning.

"Wow, this place is tidy," Tom exclaimed.

"Yeah, all Dad's doing. He's only just gone back to work today."

"What do you mean?"

"Come and sit down and I'll explain."

Nathan and Kayleesh explained everything that had happened to them since their arrival, capture and the liberation of the Earth. Tom listened in awe, before telling his own tale. He explained about the failed spotoon tour, his discovery of the mad old Luenian professor's hologram in the depths of Crossvein Tourism Centre and how he had helped Tom to contact the Radiakkan government and threaten their species. He told them of how he had then managed to make a short call via the new holoceiver as there had been a cancellation and Ghy had been happy to lend him some money so that he could check that his friends were safe. And finally, he told them how he had returned to Earth.

"We finished the spotoon tour!" he enthused. "And this time, although I was anxious to get back to you both, I could relax a bit more as I knew you were all safe and I knew that we'd defeated the Radiakkans. Hasprin's Legion recovered and Ghy brought me back here like he promised. I hope they remain in the ship until we get there though; they're not the most inconspicuous bunch. And as for where they parked the ship -"

"You played a few games of spotoon before rushing back for me?" Kayleesh gasped.

"Yes I... No, I mean..." he fumbled. Then he saw that Kayleesh was grinning. He gave her another hug and kissed her. It was the sweetest, longest kiss that he had waited for.

"I hate to break the moment," said Nathan. "But what happens now? Are you going back to Truxxe or are you going to stay here? It's just that, you're gap year is nearly over, bud."

"You're not going to leave Truxxe are you, Tom? What about the Express Cuisine? What about... *me?*"

"I... I... I don't think I can go to an ordinary English university after all of this. I've seen so much – I would be stifled being stuck inside an Oxbridge lecture hall."

"Oh, hark at him, Mister 'this planet is not big enough for me'" Nathan jested. "It wasn't that long ago that you had barely ever even ventured into the city on your own!"

"I know," Tom laughed.

"They have universities on Truxxe, you know," said Kayleesh, a sparkle in her eye.

"Of course!" yelled Tom. "There's one at Canmar Three! Do you really think that they'd take me?"

"Why don't you apply and find out? I'm sure they'd be happy to have you."

"Nathan, can I borrow your phone?"

Nathan nodded and gestured towards the land line. Tom dialled the number of his parents' home.

"Hello Mum, it's me. Yes... yes I'm fine. I just wanted to let you know that I've decided on a university. Although it's a bit of a commute..."

EPILOGUE

Tom Bowler was sitting at the front of the lecture hall, tapping notes into his portable device, as the professor dictated the highlights of the importance of Intergalactic law. It was only his third week at the institution, but Tom was already in the mind-set of a diligent student. He revelled in soaking up this new knowledge and was as enthusiastic as ever. He turned to his classmate and whispered,

"I'm so glad that you took this course too. You were wasted in the job you were doing. And you know more about the subject than anyone I know."

Gracer Menille grinned. "I'm glad too. And I could hardly carry on working on Radiakka. Even if they have promised to be a peaceful race. It just wouldn't seem right anymore."

The professor concluded the lecture and the students filed out of the building. Tom packed his portable device into his trusty rucksack and descended the slope out of the grand building, with its magnificent, metallic walls and impressive architecture. The university and central buildings were easily the most impressive in Canmar Three. They wandered across the campus green to where Kayleesh was waiting for them. She had just come out of her Multiple Language lecture and was tapping on her own device. She looked up and smiled when she noticed Tom approaching. The artificial, dream-like lighting shone on her golden hair and danced in her beaming eyes.

"How was your day?" she asked.

"Not bad," said Tom and kissed her fondly and grinned. He turned to Gracer. "Shall we see you in the student bar later then?"

"Absolutely. I wouldn't miss the inter-college spotoon match for the world!" And then she added, "plus, they're offering a new 'student special' menu from tonight; kwelps are half price - which means I can have twice as much! Oh, and I'll be bringing Marry along tonight too. She has finally fused!"

"Do you mean that Marry has matured? She's now one person?"

Gracer nodded excitedly. "It happened last night. She's beautiful. Just you wait until you see her!"

"Raphyl *will* be pleased," said Tom. He waved back at Gracer as she left the couple alone.

"Before we go," Tom said. "I remembered earlier that I still haven't given you this."

Tom reached into his pocket and disclosed a small gift.

"A paske stone pot! For me?" Kayleesh took it in her hands and ran her delicate fingers over its smooth surface. "It's beautiful!"

"Open it!" he said, excitedly. Kayleesh opened the precious pot to reveal the twinkling amber crystal. She gasped with delight and kissed Tom, passionately.

"You do know what this means don't you, Tombo?" Raphyl appeared behind him and placed a hand on Tom's shoulder.

"Er..."

"On Augtopia – the giving of a paska stone pot is a proposal of marriage!"

"It's a what?" Tom gaped, not quite sure what to do. He gazed, wide-eyed from Augtopian to Truxxian. "I didn't know... I didn't mean... not that I wouldn't, but -"

"Don't panic, Tom," Kayleesh giggled and poked Raphyl in the ribs. "He was just joking."

Relief washed over Tom and he started to laugh.

"Even after all of this, I suppose I've still got lots left to learn," said Tom.

"Well, it's a good place to start," said Raphyl, looking up at the university building, the magnificent sight of which commanded the land. "You wouldn't find me in one of those places though. It sounds far too much like hard work."

"Speaking of which, shall we get going?" suggested Tom. "That new Truxxian supervisor doesn't look as though she would tolerate lateness."

Tom Bowler, Raphyl and Kayleesh crossed the green and through the doors of the new campus eatery, the Express Cuisine II.

Hannond Putt scowled down into the huge wheelie bin, holding onto its rim with his stumpy fingers.

"I think you've done quite enough research on this planet's cuisine, Schlomm. We can leave now. I think that I've finally got the Cluock II mobile again now that the bog has dried up a little."

"I'm quite content in here, Hannond." Schlomm's voice echoed.

"So I see, but you can't spend the rest of your days sitting in a wheelie bin eating burgers which have been discarded by humans! And we can't leave The Cluock II where it is for people to find." Hannond shouted into the bin, his voice echoing around its plastic interior. Schlomm had taken residency in the service station's refuse for the past few weeks while his brother endeavoured to get the brothers space-borne again.

"Oh, I don't know Hannond – there are worse places to retire."

"Retire? What? Are you telling me that you've finally found what you claim is the tastiest meat in the universe and you don't want to get the recipe and sell our own? We could be rich!"

"Who needs money when you can have an infinite supply of barbecue sauce?" Schlomm licked his lips and chomped at a sauce-splattered burger bun. Hannond shrugged. He hoisted himself up and hopped into the bin beside him.

The lid banged shut behind him.

A few seconds later, Hannond Putt's voice echoed from within the dark bin,

"You're right, Schlomm. These are the best burgers in the universe."

"They're perfect, Hannond. Perfect indeed!" The brothers belched in unison.

ALSO BY RUTH MASTERS

THE TRUXXE TRILOGY

Three novels following the adventures of Tom Bowler, a human who finds himself working in an intergalactic service station during his gap year. He discovers the secrets of the planetoid Truxxe, traverses the galaxy to rescue his alien friend from the prison planet Porriduum and ultimately defends the earth against an alien invasion.

A cast of colourful aliens good and bad, fantastic alien worlds and witty dialogue make this trilogy a great read for any sci-fi fan!

Vol 1: All Aliens Like Burgers
Vol 2: Do Aliens Read Sci-Fi?
Vol 3. When Aliens Play Trumps

AUTOGRAPH HUNTER SERIES

A pair of "paraquels", each covering similar events, from the perspective of different characters. In both books, attendees at the same sci-fi convention happen across a real working time machine, and set off on autograph-hunting missions through time.

The two pairs of friends cross paths occasionally, with Rosemary and Joanne intriguingly being one step ahead of Alistair and Jeremy. Along the way they meet the great and the good of history, from Shakespeare to the inventor of the modern toilet. Friendships are tested and life will never be the same again…

Vol 1: Extreme Autograph Hunters
Vol 2: Ultimate Autograph Hunters

BELISHA BEACON & TABITHA TURNER

Tabitha Turner is a complaints executive from contemporary Birmingham. Belisha Beacon is a celebrity DJ working on the illustrious Möbius Strip, orbiting the planet Hayfen IV, 400 years in the future.

Inexplicably finding themselves inhabiting each other's bodies and living each other's lives the two women must survive in a strange new world.

How will they get back to their own realities… and do they want to? Nothing is ever as it seems as Belisha and Tabitha's lives begin to change forever.